Sons of a Parisian Dynasty

Claiming their legacy. Finding their family. Meeting their match!

With the retirement of their patriarch, the renowned Causcelle triplets are taking over an aristocratic empire! These gorgeous yet media-shy billionaires are stepping into the spotlight to make their mark on Paris.

Firstborn Nic has taken over the hotel branch of the business—and immediately caused a scandal with the company's new attorney! While Raoul is heading up the rest of the corporation—at least until mysteriously absent Jean-Louis can be found...

But while these brooding siblings are taking the business world by storm, their hearts are completely off-limits—when you're this wealthy, love always comes with a catch, right? Until they meet the women who show them just how wrong they are!

Find out who tames Nic in
Capturing the CEO's Guarded Heart

And see the return of Jean-Louis in
Falling for Her Secret Billionaire

Available now!

Then get ready for Raoul's story

Coming soon!

Dear Reader,

When I was young, I loved *The Nun's Story* with Audrey Hepburn. I decided I wanted to study science and work in Africa, discover something phenomenal under a microscope. But my math skills were nonexistent, so I turned to something else. I know I created this story entitled *Falling for Her Secret Billionaire* because it's about the woman I would have liked to become. She's a wonderful person.

Enjoy!

Rebecca Winters

Falling for Her Secret Billionaire

Rebecca Winters

Recycling programs
for this product may
not exist in your area.

ISBN-13: 978-1-335-73696-3

Falling for Her Secret Billionaire

Copyright © 2023 by Rebecca Winters

For questions and comments about the quality of this book, please contact us at CustomerService@Harlequin.com.

Harlequin Enterprises ULC
22 Adelaide St. West, 41st Floor
Toronto, Ontario M5H 4E3, Canada
www.Harlequin.com

Printed in U.S.A.

Rebecca Winters lives in Salt Lake City, Utah. With canyons and high alpine meadows full of wildflowers, she never runs out of places to explore. They, plus her favorite vacation spots in Europe, often end up as backgrounds for her romance novels—because writing is her passion, along with her family and church. Rebecca loves to hear from readers. If you wish to email her, please visit her website at rebeccawinters.net.

Books by Rebecca Winters

Harlequin Romance

Sons of a Parisian Dynasty

Capturing the CEO's Guarded Heart

The Baldasseri Royals

Reclaiming the Prince's Heart
Falling for the Baldasseri Prince
Second Chance with His Princess

Secrets of a Billionaire

The Greek's Secret Heir
Unmasking the Secret Prince

Escape to Provence

Falling for Her French Tycoon
Falling for His Unlikely Cinderella

Visit the Author Profile page at Harlequin.com for more titles.

I adored my doctor father, who made my life heavenly. He deserves every adulation. It's for him I dedicate this novel.

Praise for
Rebecca Winters

"This is the first book that I have read by this author but definitely not the last as it is an amazing story. I definitely recommend this book as it is so well written and definitely worth reading."

—*Goodreads* on *How to Propose to a Princess*

CHAPTER ONE

THANK HEAVEN FOR a day off from the hospital!

This Friday morning, Françoise packed up some items in her apartment in Nice to ship to a storage unit in Paris. She didn't want to have to take anything with her except a suitcase. In less than three weeks she'd be flying home to take the last of her medical boards. With luck she'd receive her doctorate.

The last item to go in the box was her father's black medical bag. He'd never had another one and it was her most prized possession. Sixty-one-year-old Patrick Valmy, who had died five months ago, had been a distinguished doctor. His fatal heart attack shouldn't have happened. Her mother, an incredible nurse who'd worked with him, had died a year before from pneumonia. She missed both of them horribly.

As she looked inside the bag one more time,

it slipped from her hands and fell upside down on the floor. Out came the percussion hammer and stethoscope she'd played with as a child.

Surprised, Françoise leaned over to pick up everything, including an old dark brown billfold. For some reason it had been lying in the bottom of the bag with everything on top of it. She'd never seen it before.

Curious, she looked inside and discovered a faded document of some kind. When she pulled it out and opened it, the first thing to catch her eye was the print at the top of the paper.

Groupe Français pour l'Adoption

Adoption? She frowned. What was this paper doing in the bottom of her father's bag? According to the information here, he'd delivered a baby. His patient's? Or someone he'd helped in an emergency?

Une enfant femelle. Née 10 Fevrier
Docteur attitré: Patrick Valmy.
Mere: inconnue
Pere: inconnue

Inconnue… Unknown.

Françoise looked down at the signatures of the adopters.

Patrick Valmy and Dionne Valmy

What?

Those were *her* parents' signatures!

They'd adopted *this* baby?

Françoise had been their only baby because her mother couldn't have more children. She'd gone through three miscarriages before Françoise's birth. If they'd adopted this child and it had died, why hadn't she known about it?

Beneath their names was the year of the adoption. Twenty-eight years ago. She'd just celebrated her twenty-eighth birthday on February 10. Françoise did the math.

No, it couldn't be!

She let out a gasp and fell back on the couch.

Something was very wrong here. She read it over and over again.

If this were to be believed, *Françoise* had been their adopted baby!

She wouldn't have cared about being adopted, but she couldn't imagine them not telling her everything. They'd had her whole life to be honest with her. Why hadn't they wanted her to know? Why the secrecy? Did they think that she would love them any less, or resent them if she'd learned the truth?

The questions kept coming. Her mother had always said she wanted more children. Why hadn't they adopted another child to give her a brother or sister? How had they kept her adoption a complete secret?

Françoise's great-aunt on her mother's side lived in a rest home at Bouzy-la-Forêt southeast of Paris. Their family had driven the two hours to visit her there on many occasions. The older woman who suffered from emphysema had never breathed a word about the adoption. Had it been so secret, her mother's *own* aunt hadn't even known?

There were no details of the baby's weight, no names of the birth parents, no city or country named, no hospital, no official stamp with the name of a functionary. Nothing she could link to anything.

Who were her birth parents? Were they still alive? If so, *where* were they?

Until now, her parents had never hurt her. But this purposely withheld information caused her more pain than she'd known in the whole of her life.

Devastated, she reached for her phone to call information and discovered there was no adoption agency with that name in Paris. She asked the operator to do a global search around France. *Nothing came up!*

Shaken to her core, she looked up the number of a private investigator here in Nice and phoned for an appointment. She asked about their fee. Though she didn't have much money, she would spend every last euro to get answers.

At two that afternoon she entered the office of Lameaux & Briand. Guillaume Briand invited her in. She showed him what she'd found and told him that no adoption agency by that name existed anywhere. "Is this even an official document?"

"I've never seen one like it, but the fact that it exists and has been hidden inside your father's medical bag must be troubling for you until we can arrive at the truth. Where did your father get his medical degree?"

"In Paris at the Sorbonne. Both my parents were Parisians, lived there and did their studies there." She gave him a full history on the family of what she knew, or *thought* she knew.

"That helps. So do the dates. You say you're twenty-eight?"

She struggled not to tear up in pain. "Yes. With the same birth date as on the document."

"Why did your parents move to Nice?"

"They didn't. Three years ago, he was invited by the French government to start a health program in Rabat for the Moroccan government. I was already a resident working on my medical degree in Paris. My parents got me enrolled at Sophia Antipolis University here in Nice so I could continue my residency and be closer to them. When I could, I visited them in Rabat and they came to me."

"I see." He removed his glasses. "I'm going to do some investigating. Leave your number and address with the secretary and I'll phone you the minute I have information."

"Thank you. I'm still shocked that my parents kept this from me." She prayed that during his search he'd discover a valid reason for what her parents had done without telling her.

"I'll do my best to get answers for you."

"Thank you." She left his office so upset she didn't know how she'd be able to function until the reason behind the adoption was uncovered.

* * *

The layout of Nice came into view as the military transport plane descended. Ten years out of the country hadn't done anything to make this moment easier, but Jean-Louis Causcelle had been discharged from the army two weeks ago and forced to return to France for medical reasons. He'd been offered a medical discharge twelve months ago but had resisted until he had no strength left to refuse.

The medic who'd done what he could to help him during the last horror in Mali couldn't tell him what was wrong. It didn't matter. Jean-Louis had been suffering with certain problems that couldn't be diagnosed in a war zone. For the last two weeks he'd sensed he was dying of some hideous disease picked up in Western Africa. He could still walk, but his recent weight loss and attacks of sickness seemed to have robbed him of strength.

There were hospitals throughout France where wounded vets could go to be treated. Since he couldn't bring himself to return to his birthplace in eastern France, he opted to fly to Nice, the home of his war buddy Alain, who'd been killed in the Sahel two months ago. Once he'd paid his respects to his best friend's family, he'd report to the vet hospital here in Nice, where he would learn how much longer he had before leaving this earth.

Once the plane landed, he got in line while an official looked through everyone's paperwork. Jean-Louis still wore his uniform, but it hung on him.

"Le prochain? Capitaine Robert Martin?"

"Ici."

Jean-Louis handed his papers to the man at the desk. Ten years ago he'd signed up for the army with a fake name. A friend had known a friend who'd helped him obtain a fake driver's license and birth certificate. He'd shaved his head and grown a moustache so he wouldn't be recognized in the photo as one of the famous billionaire Ca"scelle triplets.

Joining the army had made it possible for Jean-Louis to disappear. The deception had worked well enough to get him enlisted. However, regulations forbade facial hair, so he'd been forced to shave off the moustache.

The man stared at him for a long moment. "Now you have hair."

"My bald head made me a target. But it no longer matters." Nothing mattered.

"Soyez le bienvenu. Here is your stamped card. Show this to an official at any hospital for vets to get the treatment you need. *Bonne chance."*

Welcome home and good luck?

Right.

"Merci."

With his military career over, possibly his life, he walked out of the building on a Saturday morning in June carrying his duffel bag. He signaled for a taxi. "Darrieux Reparations Auto, 210 Rue Rossini, *s'il vous plaît."*

After climbing in, he sat back taking in the sights of a world he'd been away from for a decade. Yet it wasn't a world familiar to him. Ages ago Jean-Louis had taught himself not to think about the place his soul hungered for. To do so tortured him beyond endurance.

The driver took him along the Promenade des Anglais clustered with tourists toward his destination. The chatty man gave him a running commentary on great spots for soldiers, but Jean-Louis lost any concentration after they passed the glistening white Causcelle Prom Hotel. A nuclear bomb might as well have gone off inside him.

He closed his eyes tightly, trying to shield

himself against the invisible radiation from so many past memories. But it was too late. They penetrated to all his senses. The only reason he'd come back to France was to die.

After a few turns, the taxi came to a stop. Jean-Louis opened his eyes in time to see the small shop front where Alain had helped his father before joining the army. Both guys had been about to turn twenty. Alain's family had little money and had never traveled anywhere. He'd wanted to see the world and enjoy a different life. He'd sent part of his monthly pay to his father over the years, and the rest he'd invested for his family's future.

Jean-Louis, on the other hand, had only wanted to get away from the evil intrusion of the press and his widower father's expectations. More than that, the military had offered him a solution to become anonymous and throw off his dreadful guilt over one family having such an insane amount of money.

He and Alain met in boot camp and had served together until recently. Early death and unexpected illness hadn't figured in their plans to become career officers. Now it was time to face Alain's father and mother. Their son had worshipped them and his younger sister. That much Jean-Louis could share with their family, plus a few photos.

He asked the driver to stay put because he'd be back out again in a few minutes. Leaving his duffel bag on the seat, he walked inside the small shop wishing like hell Alain were there with that great smile on his face.

"*Salut, soldat!* What can I do to help you? Our service building is in back where the service writer will fix you up."

Jean-Louis turned to a man probably in his thirties. His nameplate said Michel. "I'm looking for the owner, Etienne Darrieux. Is he here?"

"Yes, of course. Is he expecting you?"

"No. I'd hoped to surprise him."

The man nodded. "That's his office right there." He pointed. "Just give him a heads-up."

"*Merci bien.*"

He didn't have to walk far. Alain's light brown-haired father had just gotten off the phone and looked up when Jean-Louis tapped on the doorframe. "Monsieur Darrieux? We've never met, but I'm Robert Martin, a friend of—"

He got no further because Etienne jumped out of his chair and came around to grasp

Jean-Louis in a strong hug. "I know who you are…" He spoke with deep emotion. "I can't believe you're here!"

The resemblance between father and son through coloring and facial features couldn't be denied, but it was their natural warmth that got to Jean-Louis. Meeting Etienne explained a lot. He saw framed photos of Alain on the desk.

"Please—sit down."

"I can only stay a minute. I'm due to check in at Mercy Hospital here for a full medical examination, and my taxi is waiting. But I wanted to come by first and tell you how sorry I am about Alain. He thought the world of his family. No one ever had a better friend."

Etienne's brown eyes filled with tears. Jean-Louis struggled to fight his own. "He wrote about you so much, Robert, I feel like you're part of our family."

"I know the feeling, and I have some pictures of your son I'm sure you'll enjoy." He reached in his pocket for a dozen little photos. There was much more he needed to do for Etienne if death didn't take him first.

The older man wept as he looked at them

before his head lifted. "You *have* to come back for dinner this evening. The family will want to meet you and talk to you."

"Thank you, but I won't be able to. I've been discharged from the army because I'm ill. It all depends on what the doctors tell me. It could take a while." But he doubted he'd see Etienne again. "I'll phone you."

"I'm going to hold you to that promise."

Jean-Louis left the shop. He asked the taxi driver to drive him to Mercy Hospital, where he got out at the emergency entrance with his duffel bag. Once inside, the staff processed him and took him to an examination room.

Up front the doctor on his case told him he'd have to stay at the hospital for tests for at least a week. *That long?* Jean-Louis figured he'd be dead in less time. He felt so exhausted and breathless, they moved him to a private room immediately.

Incredible but true, when the seventh day arrived after endless blood tests, X-rays and cardiograms, he realized he was still alive. "What's the verdict, Dr. Marouche? How long do I have?"

"When you came in, you said you believed you were dying, but you're not! Our epidemiologist has discovered your problem and will be in shortly to discuss it with you."

His response angered Jean-Louis. The way he felt, he couldn't imagine living any longer. "I can take bad news, and I'm not here to play word games. You don't need to pretend with me."

"I never pretend," came the sober response.

Jean-Louis didn't believe him. Since Alain's death and his illness, he'd been waiting for this pointless existence to be over. His best bud's friendship had helped compensate for the loss of his brothers, Nic and Raoul, from his life. Alain's death had compounded his grief over the loss of his family when he ran away.

Ten minutes later, a different doctor entered his room. It was a brunette wearing a mask that hid her face from view. But her white lab coat didn't prevent him from noticing her long legs and lissome body as she walked toward him. She looked attractive, as far as he could tell. Given how terrible he felt inside and out, it surprised him that she'd caught his interest at all.

Over the years in the army, he and Alain had enjoyed many women, but he'd never cultivated a long-lasting relationship. Besides his trust issues about being wanted for himself and not his money, he couldn't envision himself settling down to marriage.

His own father had lost his life's companion when Jean-Louis's mother had died in childbirth. He didn't dare put himself in the position of losing a wife. Nothing could be worth that anguish. Better to stay unattached. Safer.

It had been hard enough losing his best friend. They'd been through everything together. Alain's death had been the coup de grâce, devastating him. He'd seen too many losses in war with his own troop and with the people in Africa. He was done with it all.

"Monsieur Martin?" The woman's cultured voice forced him to pay attention. "I'm Dr. Valmy. Dr. Marouche asked me to talk to you." She moved a chair over to his hospital bed with a certain grace and sat down. He watched her pull an electronic pocket notebook from her uniform.

"He says I'm not dying. But I don't believe it when my body feels like I've just done ten rounds with a heavyweight boxer, and my head is like cotton wool. I'm twenty-nine, but I might as well be sixty."

"By your morose reply, I get the impression you wish you *were* dying." She'd said it kindly. "I can recommend an excellent psychiatrist here on staff you could talk to about your feelings."

Jean-Louis shook his head. "No thanks. I'd really prefer not to waste anyone's time. I'm not worth the trouble." As he spoke, he looked up into compassionate green eyes staring at him above her mask. They were the color of the lush grass surrounding the château on his family's estate.

"I'm sorry you feel so ill, but we're here to help you. I'll say it again. You're not dying, and if you take care of yourself, you should live a long time."

He still couldn't comprehend it. After learning of his friend's death, he'd sensed he would be next. Yet for the first time in many months, those beautiful eyes were giving him hope, something he'd thought was gone.

"I see here you joined the army at nineteen and served ten years. What I'd like you to do is think back before your military experience. Tell me if you had any of these symptoms you listed for Dr. Marouche when you were a teenager."

He blinked. "A teenager?" Her question had surprised him.

"Yes. Tell you what. I'll read each one you told him in order to jog your memory. Let's start with tiredness and weakness. When did that begin?"

"To be honest, I can't remember a time when I didn't feel that way."

"Can you give me an age?"

"Around fifteen I guess."

"You never saw a doctor about it?"

"No. After school I liked to fiddle around in the garage and just figured I never got enough sleep."

"I see. What about sweating at night?"

"I guess that's what I've been doing for years. I thought it was normal."

"Hmm. Around fifteen too?"

"Probably."

"There are other symptoms here. I'm most concerned about the difficulty you have breathing when you're lying down. Did you experience that in your teens?"

"Once or twice. When that happened, I assumed I'd caught a cold in my chest."

"Your weight loss now is understandable considering how awful you feel. You did mention blurry vision. Did that happen at school years ago?"

"I think a couple of times."

"You still said nothing to your teacher?"

"No. It went away fast. I played soccer at school. The coach warned us to drink a lot and not get dehydrated. I figured that was the reason."

She flicked him a speaking glance. "You're quite the doctor for a man with no medical training." Beneath that professional exterior, the woman had a sense of humor.

"I hated going to one."

"I understand. Most children hate it almost as much as twenty-nine-year-olds do." She had him there and he actually chuckled. "Monsieur Martin, what I've found out from the latest tests is that you have an enlarged spleen. Your answers just now verify everything. You show no signs of malaria or other illnesses you assumed you'd picked up in Africa."

"That doesn't seem possible considering I feel like the walking dead. What does an enlarged spleen signify?"

"The spleen clears blood cells from the body, but it's on overload. You have a blood disorder called polycythemia vera, or PV for short."

"I've never heard of it."

"PV occurs when there are too many red blood cells. These extra red cells make your blood thicker than normal, and the thickened blood flows slower and may clot. Red blood cells carry oxygen to organs and tissues throughout the body, so if the blood moves too slowly or clots, the cells can't deliver enough oxygen. This situation can cause the kinds of complications you've been having since you were fifteen. Left untreated, they can lead to heart disease and stroke."

He sat up in the bed. "That's truly what's wrong with me?"

"I'm positive. Twenty-two out of every one hundred thousand people have PV. But it usually hits men over sixty."

"I'm not *that* old," he murmured.

"No, you're not." She chuckled back, charming him.

"Why does it happen?"

"Because of a genetic mutation. You have one in the JAK2 gene. In most cases, PV isn't usually hereditary, but it can be passed down. I found mutations in your TET2 gene too.

PV is rarer in women. Are there any men in your family who have suffered from the same symptoms?"

"I don't have family, and I've been in the army for a decade."

"I see."

Did either of his brothers have the same problem? He prayed they didn't. The news about his condition astonished him. *He really wasn't dying?* Then that meant—that meant there was still time to make restitution for so many things. "What can be done about it, Docteur?"

"We treat it with a phlebotomy that removes blood from your body. The red blood cells contain large amounts of iron. By getting rid of the iron, the production of red blood cells by the bone marrow slows down. We'll get you started today."

"The vampire method," he muttered, but she heard him and her eyes smiled.

"Since I hope you trust me a little, *I'll* do the procedure for you this first time."

"Just to make certain I don't live forever in a different sense?" he quipped.

"Exactly. You'll die as a mortal when it's your time, that is if you follow my instructions. Give me five minutes to get what I need and I'll be back to help turn you into a new man."

"*Turn* being the operative word."

She laughed. "I may have superpowers, but would I do that to a courageous vet?"

Her friendliness had caught him unaware. He watched her womanly body leave his room and he realized he'd enjoyed talking to her. Another surprise on this day he hadn't thought could happen.

In less than five minutes she returned wearing gloves. Within seconds she'd started the procedure by inserting a needle in his left arm. "I promise this won't hurt."

She did meticulous work. Finishing up, she put a plaster over it. "How was that?"

"On a chart of one to the proverbial ten for pain, it was a zero. Thank you."

Her eyes searched his above her mask. "I'm glad to detect a change of mood in your voice. Good for the army for discharging you in time to help you get on with a new life. Not everyone is so lucky."

With that last remark, Jean-Louis sensed a kind of sadness in her tone that puzzled him.

He had an idea she was talking about herself, not him.

"We'll do this in another seven days. Just so you know, you won't be able to leave the hospital until after your next treatment because you'll need monitoring for one more week. After that, you'll have to come here every week and have this done until your red blood cell level gets closer to normal. Soon you'll start to feel much better."

"Is that a promise?"

"So, you really *do* want to live! Wonderful!" For a doctor, she had a refreshing personality and was easy to talk to. "In that case you'll need to come for a phlebotomy every three months to keep levels normal. You'll need treatment throughout your life because there is no cure, but it should be a whole long life and a rich one."

"Is that a promise too?" For the first time since losing his friend, his world had started to open up to him. Her bedside manner had everything to do with it.

"I wouldn't lie to you."

"Dr. Marouche told me the same thing."

"Out of the mouths of two witnesses," she reminded him. "I'm prescribing aspirin, which will be given to you every day for the next week. There's also a medication called hydroxyurea you take that slows the production of red blood cells. Little by little you're going to get back to normal. I wish all the patients here had a prognosis like yours. I'm sorry you don't have family who will rejoice at your good news."

But he *did* have family with brothers and sisters and a father he loved heart and soul. To have the chance to see them again...

"Take care of yourself."

Before he could tell her to wait, she walked out of the room, leaving him oddly bereft. Her intelligence and appealing nature spoke for themselves. He hadn't wanted their conversation to end, and it wasn't just because he'd found out he wasn't going to die.

The next week came and went with lots of sleep and good food. Dr. Marouche checked on him daily, but to his disappointment, there was no sign of Dr. Valmy. The rest of the time he spent on the phone putting Alain's plans for his family into action.

On the weekend he had a surprise visitor before dinner. He recognized her from some of Alain's latest photos. His sister was an attractive twenty-three-year-old with trendy short brown hair. She carried a sack in her hand. Etienne must have told her where he'd been hospitalized. The two men had talked several times on the phone in the last week.

"Capitaine Martin?"

"You have to be Suzanne."

She broke into a smile like Alain's. "Yes. Maman made you my brother's favorite *mille feuilles* and I decorated them." She put it on the bedside table. "My parents want you to come to dinner as soon as you're able."

"That's very kind of them, but I'm still undergoing tests and don't know when I'll be able to leave the hospital."

Her brown eyes wandered over him. "I'm sorry. It must be so boring for you lying here. Papa hopes when you're better you'll stay in Nice with us for a while if you don't have other plans. He'd like you to come work for him too. I work there. I'm a service writer."

"No doubt you brighten up the place. Alain told me you were the greatest sister in the world. He missed you a lot."

She nodded. "It was never the same after he left."

"I can see why. He was my best bud."

They both heard voices outside the door. "The nurse told me I couldn't stay long, and I don't want to tire you out so I'd better go."

"It means a lot to me that you came. I'll call your father when I know more. Give my best to your family and tell your mother I'll relish the *mille feuilles*. I happen to love them too. Thank you for your contribution."

"*A la prochaine*, Robert. Is it all right if I call you that?" Her unexpected visit and the hopeful look in her eyes convinced him not to get involved. Now that he didn't face a death sentence, he had other plans he'd only dreamed about. First and foremost, he needed to see his father again and hope to be forgiven for the impetuous actions that had separated him from his family for too many years.

"*Bien sûr.*"

She turned to go just as someone else came in. To his surprise it was Dr. Valmy, masked as usual. His pulse quickened. All week he'd been wondering why she hadn't been to see him. "I didn't realize you had a visitor, Monsieur Martin. How nice! I'll come back."

Dr. Valmy would have checked his daily history on the computer and knew he'd had no visitors until now.

"*Non, non.* Mademoiselle Darrieux was just leaving."

He saw Suzanne stare at the doctor and cast him a frustrated glance before disappearing. She hadn't been happy about this particular interruption.

The doctor walked closer to his bed. "You're looking healthier and more human than a week ago. Are you feeling a little better in yourself? I hope so because I came in to tell you that the latest test indicates you're not making more unwanted blood cells. That's a good sign."

She'd delivered her message, and he sensed her desire to escape, but he wanted to keep her talking. "I'll admit I have a new lease on life and have been formulating some hopefully worthwhile plans to make up for lost time."

"I'm happy to hear that." Her warmth enveloped him. It came as a surprise. He saw sincerity emanating from those lovely eyes, but he also noticed something else. It was that unexplained sense of loss in her gaze he'd seen before and it haunted him. "Just so you know, before dinner you'll be given a second phlebotomy. Antoine will be here in a minute to do the procedure."

Jean-Louis didn't want someone named

Antoine doing anything. "You're not able to?" He trusted her. *She'd* been the doctor to find out what had been wrong with him.

"I'm off duty now, but be assured, he's strictly human," she teased. "Tomorrow you can leave the hospital and do whatever you want, but come back in one week. The staff at the front desk will arrange all your appointments from now on. If you have any problems, get in touch with Dr. Marouche, your doctor of record. *Bonne nuit, monsieur.*"

CHAPTER TWO

Jean-Louis hadn't wanted Dr. Valmy to leave yet, but over the years he'd grown used to losses. Since he wouldn't be staying in Nice, saying good-night to her also meant saying goodbye. He'd always been able to walk away from a woman. For the first time ever, that didn't sit well with him.

A few minutes later Antoine appeared. He was a talker who told him he was a med student. He had a brother in the air force and chatted with Jean-Louis for a long time after his blood was taken. The conversation eventually turned into a discussion of Dr. Valmy, who he learned was here on a fellowship. Antoine was crazy about her and he was a fountain of knowledge.

The brilliant epidemiologist, daughter of a renowned Parisian doctor now deceased, had turned down every guy working at the hospital, including Antoine. Hospital gossip said she was involved with one of the men on the French trade commission to Morocco. The man had distinguished himself and was headed for an illustrious career that might include running for the president of France.

Apparently, this man was a Moreau whose family lived in one of the famous Auteuil villas of the nineteenth century in Paris. Before leaving for military service, Jean-Louis had known of their family. It would probably be the marriage of the season.

He'd thought Dr. Valmy was a Niçoise and about twenty-four years old. But with all her schooling, she had to be a few years older. She might not have a ring on her finger yet, but it sounded like it was going to happen. The news disturbed him in ways he didn't want to examine. Poor Antoine.

As for Jean-Louis, he needed to make up for lost time. Ten years' worth. The next morning, he left the hospital with his duffel bag. Before he did anything else, he hailed a taxi to drive him to the bank to withdraw some funds accrued from his army pay. From there he checked into a hotel and went out to buy some casual clothes. The rest of the day he worked on the plans Alain had shared with Jean-Louis. It was up to him to carry them out.

On the following day, he took a taxi to the Darrieux body shop. Alain had cried to him many times over abandoning his father and mother after joining the army. But he'd died before he could be with his family again. No one understood how that felt like Jean-Louis did. Now that he knew he was destined to live, he wanted to act for Alain and help out his best friend before leaving Nice.

Etienne looked up from his desk in surprise. "Robert—"

The two men hugged. Jean-Louis sat down. "I hope you have some time for me, Etienne."

"I'll make time. You look much better."

"I'm feeling better and I'm here for a specific reason. I have a present for you from your son."

"A present?"

"You'll have to come with me to see it. He said you've wanted it for at least thirty-five years. It was a dream of yours."

The older man squinted like he couldn't understand.

"Let's go and I'll show it to you." They left

in the taxi and drove to a big Ferrari dealership about a mile away. It took up a lot of the block. A huge sign towered over it with the name Etienne Darrieux. He watched the older man's expression. His head jerked around.

"What is this? Some kind of joke?"

"Not at all. Your son has been paying for it since he was deployed. He planned to help you run it after he got out of the army. He felt terrible that he'd been gone so long and couldn't wait to go into business with you."

Etienne shook his head. "He never had that kind of money."

Jean-Louis had secretly mined his own wealth and connections to seal the deal, but Etienne would never know that. "He earned it month after month. Four months ago, he put it all in your name. Let's go inside and meet the manager, Jules Villon. He'll have all the banking and paperwork to show you signed by your son."

He scratched his head. "You're putting me on."

"I swear I'm not." Jean-Louis got out of the car and Etienne followed.

They no sooner walked in the front door and the manager walked up to them. "I've been waiting to meet the new owner. I'm Jules." He shook both their hands. "I understand you have a body shop over on Rue Rossini, Monsieur Darrieux. Are you keeping that too?"

"I don't believe this is happening," he murmured to Jean-Louis, who hoped his deceased friend could see his father's happiness now. They spent the next two hours going over the books. Jules gave Etienne a tour of the whole place and he met the employees. When he returned to the office looking dazed, Jean-Louis got up. He felt a joy beyond words to have fulfilled Alain's wish.

"I have to get back to the hotel, so if you want to stay here longer, I'll call for a ride, but I promise to stay in touch."

"No, no. We'll take a taxi to my shop together." Etienne was so overcome, he wept. En route, he thanked Jean-Louis profusely. When the taxi pulled up in front, Etienne got out. "What are your plans?"

"Tomorrow I'm renting a car and taking a trip to see the country. I haven't been behind the wheel of a car since I was nineteen." He needed to put substance to ideas that had been percolating since Dr. Valmy had assured him he'd live a long life. Home was his ultimate destination. "I won't be back, but I'll keep in touch with you."

"Please keep me posted, Robert. You're like a second son."

Jean-Louis felt touched to the core. "That means more to me than you'll ever know. You're like family to me too, and one day we'll see each other again."

"Where are you going now?"

"Back to the Excelsior Hotel, where I stayed last night."

Etienne tried to hand him some money, but he refused. "I've saved my pay. No worry there, but thank you."

Jean-Louis saw the question in the older man's eyes that he'd never put to words. *What about your family, Robert?* It was a question he couldn't answer yet because it was too painful. After he'd seen his family, then he'd tell Etienne the truth.

"*Dieu vous protégé*, Etienne. You're the best man I know."

Except for my father, but I learned that truth far too late.

They hugged once more before he told the driver where to head. After he got dropped off at a café near the hotel and had dinner, he walked back. No sooner did he reach his room on the second floor when he heard a pounding on the door. Actually, he heard separate poundings, both insistent. Was the hotel on fire or something? He hadn't heard an alarm.

"Monsieur Martin? *Ouvrez la porte, vite!*"

He rushed to open it.

Two mirror images of himself stood before him. He thought he was going to pass out and stepped back in shock.

"*Grâce à Dieu* we've found you!"

Jean-Louis had no defense against his own tears as his brothers broke down with him. They all kept hugging each other and thanking God for this miracle.

To be with Raoul and Nic again… It was too much. He couldn't handle it and fell back in the sofa, burying his face in his hands while his body heaved with happy sobs. He finally lifted his tear-stained face. "How in heaven did you find me?"

Raoul smiled. "With the help of a retired secret service agent named Claude Giraud and a lot more from above. He found out a Robert Martin had been at boot camp ten years ago and became best friends with an Alain Darrieux. But out of all the enlistees, he could find no proof that a Robert Martin had ever existed before signing up. Then he discovered that both of you were master mechanics. You had already earned that reputation at home."

Nic nodded. "That gave him his second clue and from there he identified the forger who made up your documents. He also learned that Alain died two months ago and soon after, you were discharged from the army for illness. It's obvious you've lost weight and look drained. We've been desperately worried since learning the truth."

"I feel a whole lot better than I did two weeks ago. You should have seen me then."

"We're glad you're getting better, but why were you so sick?" Raoul questioned.

"I have a blood disorder called polycythemia vera that doesn't have to be fatal, but I make too many red blood cells. Some of my blood has to be drawn once a week and eventually every three months to stay healthy. I'll explain in detail later, but I'm feeling better and want to hear how Claude caught up to me."

"He traced you to Nice," Raoul explained. "All he had to do was flash your photo at

Alain's sister in his father's shop and she identified you at once. Robert Martin is a big name around there."

He shook his head in wonder. "Do they know who I really am yet?"

"Nope. We told Claude why you joined up in the first place. He would never give you away."

Relief swept through him. He wanted to be the one to tell Etienne the truth.

"Is Alain's sister someone special?" Nic teased with a gleam in his eyes.

It looked like he had Suzanne to thank for a positive identification, but Jean-Louis wasn't complaining. He'd been through too much. After seeing Etienne's pain over the loss of his son, he was tired of running away from his life.

"Only special enough for your super sleuth to have figured out my deception. I'm thankful he did." He stared at the two of them. "Tomorrow I'd planned to drive home to see all of you, and here you are. I can't believe I'm not dreaming."

"We can't either." They both hunkered down in front of him. Nic looked into his eyes. "With you gone, life's never been the same for us or our sisters, and definitely not for our father. *Frérot?* It's why we hired Claude to find you."

Raoul gripped his arm. "Papa hasn't been well and yearns to see you. His pain over the way he treated you ten years ago has plagued him. He's wanted to see you again and ask for your forgiveness."

Jean-Louis moaned. *He* was the one who needed to ask, *beg* his father to forgive him for being such an ungrateful son. To his joy it *wasn't* too late. With maturity he realized his flight from home had been rooted in a teenage rebelliousness against circumstances that weren't anyone's fault.

No one could have prevented his mother's death. Their family's obscene wealth had its naissance centuries earlier. His father had only tried to preserve that legacy. Certainly Jean-Louis's responsibility for a troop of soldiers had opened his eyes to the challenges his father had to overcome to raise their large family alone.

"We flew here in the family jet and want to take you to La Racineuse tonight before more time passes. Two months ago the doctor made him retire. He has a medical helper named Luca. Corinne moved into the château with Gaston and the kids, but everyone is trying to take care of him," Raoul explained.

Jean-Louis started to tremble. "What's wrong with him?"

"Heart disease," they said at the same time.

He remembered a question Dr. Valmy had asked him about any male in his family who suffered from the same symptoms. His brothers seemed well enough. *Had his father developed PV over the years?*

"My life hasn't been the same since either. I need to see him more than you'll ever know." He got to his feet. "I'm ready to go right now. Let me throw my stuff in my duffel bag." While in La Racineuse, he'd go to the hospital there and have his blood drawn. But he wished Dr. Valmy would be there to do it.

He'd only met her twice, yet her warmth and sincerity had drawn him to her. She'd helped him with his depressive thoughts in a straightforward and compassionate manner. Putting all that together, combined with a compelling physical attraction despite the fact he'd never seen her without her mask, and he couldn't get her off his mind. After he'd paid his hotel bill, they went out to a waiting limo that drove them to the airport. Once on board they congregated in the lounge compartment and the jet took off. Jean-Louis didn't know the pilot or steward. Too much time had gone by, but the new staff recognized the missing triplet and went out of their way to welcome him home.

Maybe his eyes deceived him. "Nic? Is that a wedding ring I see?"

His brother grinned. "I married the woman of my dreams three weeks ago. She's the attorney Papa hired right before he had to retire. One look at her and that was it for me."

"Felicitations!"

"We're building a home in Roselin Woods as we speak."

"That's what we named it when we found all those finch nests that day on our bike ride."

"That was one fun day."

So much life had gone on without him. He turned to Raoul. "What about you?"

"I haven't been lucky like Nic." His brother averted his eyes and his face clouded over. Jean-Louis realized this wasn't the moment to question him.

"There's too much trouble going on at La Racineuse," Raoul explained.

"What do you mean? Don't tell me old man Dumotte is still doing his worst?"

"Worse than his worst," Nic broke in.

"How is that possible?"

His brothers looked at each other. "We have some sad news. Oncle Raimond died of ALS the night I got married," Nic informed him.

"I loved that man," Jean-Louis murmured.

"We all did. Papa asked Raoul to leave the corporation we were running together and come home to run the estate. He's doing what he was always meant to do. But the second Dumotte found out, he went into a meltdown and burned one of the barns in protest."

"I knew it!" Jean-Louis blurted. "He's always hated Papa. The man's irrationality has finally turned him into a maniac." He looked at Nic. "I take it you must be running the whole corporation in Paris now."

"No. I help when I can, but to my joy Causcelle is now in the hands of our inimitable cousin Pascal and Papa's assistant George Delong."

"There never was anyone like him!" Jean-Louis cried. "He was always my favorite cousin."

"Everyone likes Pascal. You'd think he was born to it."

"Another Papa?"

Both brothers nodded.

"Then what are *you* doing, Nic? Besides being a new euphoric husband, of course." The look in Nic's eyes confirmed his happiness. How would it be to have found the love of his life and experience that kind of joy? For the first time in years, Jean-Louis began to think marriage might be something to aspire to rather than reject. Nic's delight and contentment was real, and once again unbidden thoughts of Dr. Valmy entered Jean-Louis's mind.

For the next few hours he listened as his brothers caught him up on everything that had gone on over the years. Nic went into detail about the reconstruction of the church where their mother's brother Gregoire had died in a fire years ago.

He explained about the free hospital/hotels he wanted built around France, secretly in honor of Gregoire and the other monks who'd lost their lives. This first one would include a bovine research center, but all of it was still in the planning stage.

"You should have gone into science, Nic." He knew his brother's heart.

"That's old ground now."

Shivers raced through Jean-Louis's body. He couldn't believe what his brother had just told him. Nic's ideas coincided very much with his own future dreams that had developed while he'd been in the hospital. Maybe this was a triplet thing to be on the same wavelength. But it was something he'd talk about with them later.

The Fasten Seat Belts sign flashed, bringing their conversation to an end. The plan was to drive the fifteen miles from Chalon Champforgeuil airport to the château where his old bedroom had been waiting for him. He felt intense remorse over the childish anger that had caused him to run away from his birthright, from all that had been precious to him.

He owed everything to his father, who'd had to go it alone when their mother had died in childbirth. He'd be home soon to see the whole family and embrace his beloved parent. He wanted to make up for so much while there was still time with his father.

Jean-Louis no longer gave a damn about

being recognized as one of the world-famous triplet billionaire sons. Like Nic, he planned to turn all of it to the good. Even better, Raoul had gone back to the estate he'd never wanted to leave. Happiness was possible for all of them.

What was it Dr. Valmy had said to him? *So, you do want to live!* She had no idea… His only problem was that he found himself thinking about her way too much. But right now his thoughts were on the father he hadn't seen for years.

The drive to the château didn't take long. As soon as they drove up, Jean-Louis leaped out of the car and hurried inside to look for his father. He found him on the terrace at the rear of the château sitting in a wheelchair. His caregiver smiled and nodded to him.

A boulder had lodged in his throat. "Papa?"

His father stirred, then looked over at him. "Jean-Jean, *mon fils.*" He called him by his nickname and threw out his arms to him. Jean-Louis ran into them and they hugged for a long, long time. Both men wept.

"Forgive me for leaving you, *mon père.* I love you and have missed you so much."

"There's nothing to forgive. I thank God

you've come home and that your life has been preserved. That's all I've ever wanted. I love you, Jean-Jean."

"It's heaven to be home. I'll never leave you again."

Today had been Françoise's last day at Mercy Hospital. She'd done her packing and tomorrow she would be leaving for Paris. As she got ready to walk out of the lab for the last time, she received a call and prayed it was Guillaume Briand. Her concerns over the adoption had grown more troubling while she'd been waiting for news from him.

To her consternation it was Eric who wanted to explain that he couldn't fly to Nice this weekend because of official business in Rabat. He was terribly upset and promised to make it up to her in Paris in a few weeks.

That phone call was an answer to prayer.

Their relationship should never have happened. When he contacted her in Paris, she would have to tell him goodbye. They'd met at her father's funeral in Paris and he'd started dating her after she'd flown back to Nice, but her attraction to him hadn't grown. She knew it was time to stop seeing him.

Her boards couldn't have come at a better time. She wasn't in love with him, and finding that hidden adoption record had turned her inside out so she couldn't concentrate on anything else. Her fear now was to try not to fail her exam while she waited for news from Monsieur Briand.

Suddenly Antoine rushed in to say goodbye. She could tell something was wrong. "What's on your mind?"

"Besides your leaving?"

She smiled at the younger man. "You knew it had to happen, but I'll miss you too. Now tell me what's wrong."

"I did all the lab work for today's patients, but our army vet didn't show."

That caught her off guard. "Maybe he came yesterday."

He shook his head. "Nope. No one has seen him all week. He never kept his appointment."

"That's not good."

"I talked to Dr. Marouche. He's worried our patient might have had a serious death wish and didn't want answers."

There'd been a time when she'd thought the same thing. Antoine's comment about Dr. Marouche confirmed it. "He said that?"

"More or less. I liked Robert."

Liked wasn't the right word when she thought of her patient. The first night after she'd met him, she'd had a dream about him that still shocked her. She was glad to be leaving for Paris, where she wouldn't be seeing him again. It haunted her even now.

"I'm sure he'll show up soon, Antoine. Maybe he's been too sick to come."

"Maybe."

"He had one visitor who might be looking after him and will see that he comes."

"You think?"

"Yes." Françoise had to admit it wasn't possible for a woman to ignore Robert, certainly not the one who came to his room the other day. She'd seen the hungry look in the young woman's eyes. Despite his illness, he was unusually attractive and possessed an intriguing personality. His sense of humor had made her laugh. To think he'd managed to get through twenty-nine years of life doctoring himself.

Françoise found it miraculous that he had such an amazing constitution and strength of will considering his PV. But lurking in the black recesses of his eyes, she'd seen hurt and sorrow. She couldn't be sure if war had done that to him, or something, or…someone. Both she and Dr. Marouche had gotten the idea he'd been welcoming death until he was told he was going to live and why. The change in him had fascinated her, as if the words had pulled him out of a terrible nightmare.

Remembering that illuminating moment after she'd told him he'd live a long life, she said to Antoine, "I'm sure he doesn't have a death wish now. Don't give up on him."

She kissed his cheek. "*A bientôt*, Antoine. Take care of yourself. I know for a fact dozens of girls are out there waiting for you to date them." No doubt there were thousands of them waiting for Robert when he'd recovered. "Email me when you meet *the one*, and bring her to Paris so I can meet her."

"I'll do that, and I know you'll ace your boards."

"Let's hope so."

She grabbed her purse and hurried out in front of the hospital to get a taxi.

No sooner had she given the driver the address of her apartment than her phone rang. Seeing the ID, she clicked on immediately. "Monsieur Briand? I'm so glad it's you. Please tell me you have good news for me."

"I'm afraid not. This is a case that has been specially sealed in the strictest legal sense."

Her spirits plunged. "What do you mean *specially*?"

"It means it contains information that mustn't come to light under any circumstances."

She could hardly breathe. "In other words…"

"In other words, there's nothing more I can do," he affirmed in a serious tone. "It isn't a case of needing more money. I'm so sorry."

"So am I," she said in a tortured whisper. "Thank you for all your help."

"It's been my pleasure, Dr. Valmy."

Françoise hung up in a stupor.

She knew nothing about her birth parents and the kind of people they were. She never would. Did she have other siblings? Grandparents? Aunts and uncles? So many questions haunted her. She couldn't conceive of her adoptive father and mother hiding this from her and was shattered by it.

It was a good thing she wasn't in love with Eric because she realized she wouldn't be having a relationship with any man unless she got answers.

What if her birth mother or father had some

kind of inherited disease or a psychiatric disorder that could have been passed on to her? Had her adoptive parents decided not to let her know anything because she'd shown no signs yet? How could she ever marry or have children if such a thing were a possibility?

Equally horrible, what if it turned out her father—lauded by the government for his contribution to medicine—had done something to ruin his stellar reputation? If that delivery had been on the up and up, there'd have been no need to hide it from her forever.

Torn apart by too many ugly thoughts, she made up her mind that once she'd passed her boards—*if she did*—she'd leave Paris and go someplace where her adoptive father hadn't been known. All these years everyone had commented about her inheriting her father's fabulous genes. Nothing could be further from the truth.

She didn't know the identity of her birth father or mother. Finding that adoption paper had robbed her of her identity as a Valmy. All of her life she'd taken such pride in her family history and lineage. The hidden document made her feel like she'd just been born.

Welcome to a world where her birth parents could be out there. Did they wonder or worry about her? Life as she'd known it had turned into a nightmare.

After two and a half weeks in Paris to convince the jury, Françoise had just received her doctorate. She could claim it officially, but the phone call from Guillaume Briand in Nice might as well have slammed her through a wall.

She hadn't been the same since he'd discovered that the adoption case had been specially sealed under the law. In his opinion it meant something did have to be concealed. Unfortunately, there was no way ever to learn the facts.

Feeling as if she'd been permanently frozen in a void, it was a miracle she'd gotten through her exams.

"Dr. Valmy?"

She looked up from the computer. "Christophe!" The married, sixty-year-old head of epidemiology known professionally as Dr. Soulis had just left his private office in the lab on the fifth floor of The Good Shepherd Hospital in Paris. He'd been in touch with her for the last year and was responsible for hiring her the moment he knew she'd received her degree.

He winked at her. "It's good to have another Valmy back at the helm. Your father was a legend around here before he left us to serve France in Morocco. Now that you're here, all is forgiven. We expect wonders from you."

She groaned inwardly. "Are you trying to terrify me after my third day on the job?"

"You're his daughter. What is there to fear?"

"You don't want to know."

He laughed and said good-night before disappearing out the door. How lucky for her to be working under someone so likeable and pleasant, but not for long. The sealed adoption had changed everything. Once she'd found another hospital position far from Paris where her father hadn't been known, she'd turn in her notice.

As she studied the latest case, Celestine, the young clerk at the fifth-floor desk, came rushing into the lab. "Dr. Valmy?"

"Yes? Right here."

"Oh, good." She ran over to her. "I saw Dr. Soulis leave and was afraid you might have gone home too."

"Is there a problem?"

"A man came in at the last minute for blood work. He didn't have an appointment. I told him he was too late, but I thought I'd check one more time."

"I'm just leaving, Celestine." Eric had flown into Paris today and would be coming over to her apartment tonight to celebrate her graduation. She dreaded it, but she had to break off with him. "Will you tell the patient to come back tomorrow at ten and one of the staff will take care of him?"

"Yes, of course. Ooh, I wish I were a phlebotomist."

"You can certainly train to become one."

"That isn't what I meant."

"I don't understand."

"He's the hunkiest man I ever saw in my life and he's a vet! I didn't know there were men like him in existence! See you on Monday." She rushed out.

"*A bientôt*, Celestine."

Back in Nice, Françoise had also met a hunky vet, one who'd infiltrated her mind in a dream she needed to get out of her head. Maybe looking for a new car to buy tomorrow would help erase him from her thoughts.

After years of commuting by bus and taxi, she looked forward to having her own transportation no matter where she ended up. Eric would have picked her up, but she didn't want to be beholden to him in any way.

She closed the file and removed her uniform. Beneath it she'd worn one of her work blouses and skirts. After grabbing her purse, she left the lab for the elevator down the hall. As she stepped in, a woman and man followed. She'd assumed they were together until the woman got off on the third floor.

After reaching the main floor, she got out first and headed for the entrance. Once outside the busy hospital, she waited at the *tête de taxi* for a ride. If one didn't come soon, she'd phone for one.

Several cars drove past coming out of the parking lot. A black Mercedes actually stopped in front of her and an incredibly handsome man at the wheel got out. He walked toward her. She felt his eyes studying her. "Excuse me. Is it possible you're Dr. Valmy?"

"Yes, but—" She'd been going to say she didn't recognize him. Then she looked into those compelling black eyes that were so familiar. "Monsieur Martin!"

"Yes, I'm Robert, your former patient in Nice. The one whose life you saved and promised would live for a long time. I thought it was you in the elevator, but I never saw you without your mask on until today."

This man *couldn't* be the same one, but he was. "It *is* you. *You're* the patient who wanted your blood drawn here a little while ago?"

"How did you know that?"

"Because I work at this hospital now. The clerk said a vet had come without an appointment, but I was on the verge of leaving. If I'd known it was you, I would have taken care of you. I'm so sorry when you took all the trouble to come here."

"No problem. It's my fault. I got so busy today, I didn't make an appointment. I'd hoped I could get it done before going to my hotel. It doesn't matter. I'll come again tomorrow morning. Why are you in Paris?"

"Paris is my home. I came to take my final boards and now I'm employed here."

He rubbed the back of his neck. "I thought you were from Nice."

"Only living there for the last three years. When my parents moved to Rabat for a government assignment, I worked at Mercy Hospital in Nice to do my residency and fellowship through Sophie Antipolis University. That way I could see my parents more often."

"Now I understand, but I have to admit I'm surprised to find you here."

"It's a surprise for me too." He was the embodiment of the man in her dream. "Before I left Nice, Antoine told me you didn't come in for your phlebotomy. What happened to you? I had no idea I'd see you here."

"I've been in the east of France and received treatments at another hospital there."

"Well, it shows. In just a month you seem healthier. It's amazing what those treatments along with nourishing food and rest have done for you."

"You promised I'd get better," he said with a smile.

She'd never seen him in anything but a hospital gown because he'd always been in bed. The tall, rock-solid man who had to be six foot three was dressed in a pullover and jeans. In a word, he looked sensational.

The two times she'd been in his room, he'd appeared down and out. Clean shaven now with vibrant black hair, she found his transformation astounding. He no longer resembled a wounded animal. She saw life in those black eyes that hadn't been there before.

Just then a taxi pulled up to the *tête de taxi.* "It looks like I've got a ride. That's good because I have plans and need to get home. I've enjoyed seeing you again, Robert, and am so glad you're doing well." She feared she'd be dreaming about him again tonight.

"Please wait a moment, Dr. Valmy. After what you've done for me, I want to repay you for saving my life. That's not lip service," he claimed in a more serious tone of voice. "Would you consider letting me give you lunch at my hotel tomorrow? It would mean a lot to me. Circumstances in Nice prevented me from talking to you one more time. We might never see each other again. Please say yes."

Like Antoine, she liked Robert. How could she possibly say no? "Since you were turned away from getting your blood drawn, I'd enjoy lunch with you. But it will have to be a late one since I'm buying a new car tomorrow."

His eyes held a gleam. "Then let's say four o'clock. Will that give you time to negotiate the sale and try out your new purchase to your heart's content?"

She smiled at him. "So you know what that's like."

"Oh, yeah. There's nothing more fun."

"I've never owned my own car and I'm really excited."

"I'm excited for you. Do you have a make in mind?"

"None that I can afford."

He laughed. "Then it will keep me guessing until you arrive."

"I'll try to get there on time. Thank you. By the way, where is there?"

A chuckle escaped. "23 Marais Place. I'll be out in front to meet you." He walked over to the taxi. After saying something to the driver, he opened the rear door for her. "Don't take too many chances. There are other sick people in desperate need of your particular services. You're a rarity and I for one will always be grateful. Your diagnosis brought me back to life, and this chance meeting allows me to do something for you in return."

She felt his sincerity to her bones. "You're very kind." And too appealing for her own good. "*A demain*, Robert."

The drive to the apartment that the hospital had arranged for her to live in didn't take long. Meeting him had been a surprise that shouldn't have thrilled her so much. He'd put her in a different mood as she got ready for Eric to come over. Robert's words of appreciation had been a balm to her soul even if she didn't know her true origins or destiny.

Now it was time to do the one thing she *could* do something about. Eric deserved his freedom even if he didn't know it yet. He was a terrific man, but not the one for her.

A half hour later she heard the knock on the door. When she opened it, dark-haired Eric swept her into his arms and kissed her hungrily. "I thought this day would never come. You aced your exams. Now we can get engaged and plan our wedding."

She eased herself away from him and walked in the living room. "Eric?" Françoise turned to him. "Sit down for a minute so we can talk. I've enjoyed our times together very much, but the truth is, I can't marry you. It hurts me to say it, but for the last month I've tried to be honest with you so you'd understand."

His features creased in confusion. "What

do you mean you can't?" He hadn't been listening to her. "I understood your hesitation before your exams, but now—"

"Now it's truth time," she cut him off. "I'm not in love the way I need to be in order to marry you."

His brown eyes looked incredulous. "I don't believe you're saying that to me."

"I know, and I'm so sorry. I tried to tell you before."

"There's someone else."

"No. No one." Her dream had nothing to do with reality. "Something has held me back from committing. Time away from you has made me realize how I really feel."

He shook his head. "You've been alone too much since the deaths of your parents. You aren't yourself. We need more time together. I'll call you tomorrow. We'll drive out to the house I want to buy for us and we'll really talk before I have to get back to Morocco. I have big plans about my campaign, and they include you."

"It won't work, Eric." She paused. "In fact, I'm not sure I'll ever get married." She meant it.

"That's crazy."

"No, it's not, but I have my reasons. I don't

want to be cruel to you. You're a marvelous man, but I can't do this anymore. Please try to understand. And right now, I'm very tired and need to get to bed."

He got up and came over to kiss her cheek. "Be warned. I'm not letting you get away from me."

She knew he was in pain, but one day he'd meet a woman who would make him happy. Françoise couldn't be that person.

CHAPTER THREE

THE NEXT MORNING Françoise took a hot shower and washed her hair. To her relief she hadn't dreamed, but that was probably because she'd be seeing Robert before the day was out.

Normally she'd wear pants and a top. But because he'd invited her for a meal, she chose to dress up a little and wear her blue-and-white-print sundress. It had the same print on the short-sleeved jacket. She brushed her hair and put on some pink frost lipstick. After slipping on white sandals, she felt ready to go.

By three o'clock Françoise had bought a metallic blue Nissan Versa she liked and felt she could afford. After driving it around overjoyed, she did a few errands and headed for Robert's hotel in the Marais district. She'd been away from Paris for three years and welcomed the familiar sights with all its older charm and glory from past kings.

In another few minutes she slowed down to turn into the courtyard of a modernized two-story palace with a fountain she'd passed many times over the years. It had never been open to the public.

Françoise knew she'd come to the right address, but this palace couldn't be a hotel. There had to be one behind it. She wound around, but saw nothing except some security guards at the entrance. Hopefully, they could tell her where to find it. After parking, she got out and heard footsteps.

When she turned around, there stood Robert. Instead of casual clothes, he wore an expensive-looking light blue suit with white shirt and tie. For a second, Françoise couldn't think as she studied the chiseled features that made him the best-looking man she'd ever seen in her life. Those black eyes gleamed beneath luxuriant jet-black hair.

"I'm crazy about the color of your car, Dr. Valmy. A Nissan is always dependable. That's important considering you're a doctor. Congratulations on your choice."

"Thank you. I love it. But tell me something. I thought you said this was a hotel."

He nodded. "It is. However, everyone who stays here calls it the *palais*. Shall we go in?"

She walked inside with him. He called to the guard at the front desk. "I don't want to be disturbed, Guy."

By whom?

He cupped her elbow and walked her down the hall and around a corner to another wide corridor. They soon came to an elevator and rose to the next floor. She experienced more surprises when the door opened into the foyer of an elegant suite.

Her host walked her into the salon with its sumptuous furnishings and floor-to-ceiling windows. She noticed the intricately paneled walls—this had been a palace after all, but it had a comfortable, inviting feeling you didn't often associate with such a magnificent building. How had he obtained permission to be here? He'd been a mystery from the first. That hadn't changed.

"The restroom is down the hall on the right. Go ahead and freshen up first."

When she came back to the salon, she found him waiting for her. He'd removed his suit jacket. "Sit down, Dr. Valmy."

"Thank you. Please call me Françoise."

"I'd like that." He sat on an upholstered chair. "After our talk, we'll have dinner in the dining room."

"A talk?" What did he mean?

"I want you to understand the depth of my appreciation for you. I wouldn't be alive if it weren't for you. Please let me get this off my chest."

"I'm glad I happened to be the doctor who discovered your problem, but let's not make more of it. Any epidemiologist would have found it."

"That isn't what Antoine told me, and I need to unburden myself to you."

Once again, she found herself concerned by that pained expression in his eyes. "What's wrong?"

"When I was your patient for that brief period in Nice, I lied to you about certain aspects of my life. Since seeing you yesterday, I know I must tell you the whole truth. The first thing I want you to know is that my name isn't Robert Martin."

Françoise had found a place on the end of the damask-covered couch and folded her arms, trying to relax. It proved impossible when his

admission had surprised her. First her parents'
sin of omission. Now his.

He leaned forward with his hands on his
powerful legs. "I've got a picture to show you.
It may explain a lot, then again, maybe nothing."

"Where is it?"

"On the coffee table in front of you."

She hadn't noticed the framed five-by-
seven photo lying facedown next to the vase
of flowers.

"Go ahead and take a look at it."

She reached for it and discovered a black-
and-white picture. What she saw were three
young handsome guys with black hair. They
all looked like Robert, who'd said he wasn't
Robert Martin. All were dressed in the same
pants and pullovers with the name Racine
Rams imprinted from their high school. They
were triplets! How incredible. She studied the
picture for a minute. *Racine Rams.*

Wait a minute… *Triplets!*

All of a sudden she remembered hearing about a famous set of triplets before her
parents moved to Morocco three years ago,
taking her to Nice to be near them. They'd
been a year older than she and were the sons

of a multi-multi-billionaire who'd lost their mother. Their pictures had been all over the media and the news, and her girlfriends had been gaga over them. What was their father's name? She searched her brain. Over time she'd lost track, but seeing this photo brought it all back.

She felt dark eyes on her. "You're a brilliant doctor, and I can see it's on the tip of your tongue." He could read her mind.

"I've almost got it. Don't tell me."

He chuckled. "Take your time. We've got all night."

"Something *scelle*. Porscelle? No. Borscelle."

"Try starting with the first letter of the alphabet."

"Aurscelle?"

"Keep going." His smile had turned into a grin.

"I've done *A* and *B*. That leaves *C* next. Corscelle," she blurted.

"Close," he quipped.

She jumped to her feet and walked around looking at the photo. "Conscelles."

He shook his head.

"Curscelles."

"Je regrette..." he teased.

"Oh, why can't I think of it?"

The man who had called himself Robert sat back in the chair putting his hands behind his head. He was so attractive, it shouldn't be allowed. "Think of the Promenade des Anglais in Nice."

She nodded. "I've walked along there hundreds of times."

"In that case, why don't we eat our meal while it's hot. I'm sure it will come to you in time."

"I can't until I've solved this."

"You're probably a whiz at crossword puzzles."

"My roommates have hated me for it. My mother was the only person who could beat me." *My adoptive mother.*

"So, you inherited your smarts from both sides of your family."

She'd inherited everything from her birth parents. Who they were? She didn't know and never would. "Maman was smart enough to marry my father. Why aren't I smart enough to come up with the name I'm looking for?"

"You're trying too hard."

"You're right." She stopped and looked at the

picture again, then flicked him another glance. "The Promenade des Anglais, huh?"

"Plain as the lovely nose on your face."

She shrugged her shoulders in defeat. "I know you're hungry, so I give up."

"I can wait."

"No, you can't. I heard your stomach growl."

At that comment, rich male laughter poured out of him. "I'll give you one more hint. Think of a celebrity hotel."

Celebrity...

Suddenly the light dawned. "The Causcelle Prom Hotel!"

He stood to his full height. "You got it in six. *Bravo!*"

By now the blood had started to drain from her face and she felt light-headed. "*You're* one of the world-famous Causcelles—do you know the odds of that happening? Which one are you?"

"Jean-Louis."

"I think I'm going to faint."

He rushed over and put her on the sofa, pushing her head down. The picture fell to the floor. When the world stopped spinning, she lifted her head and stared at him. "It's my turn to owe *you*, Monsieur Causcelle. If

I'd fallen, I would probably have cracked my head open."

"At least I'm good for something." He still had his hand on the back of her neck. One of his fingers played absently with a curl, sending darts of awareness through her.

Françoise couldn't stop looking at him. "You're the missing son everyone used to wonder about." The man in my dream.

He smiled. "They still do."

"Jean-Louis. Good heavens. You have a fabulous heritage with a family tree that goes back centuries! I remember now." She couldn't believe it. "And here you thought you were dying. They must be overjoyed beyond belief that you're back." Françoise envied that he knew without a doubt who'd parented him.

"I'm still trying to take it all in. Your diagnosis turned my world around. That's because you're the genius daughter of a renowned doctor. Genes don't lie. Antoine bragged about you and I can see why."

Françoise averted her eyes. "I had no idea Antoine was a walking encyclopedia."

"The man's in love with you, that's why." She'd suspected Antoine cared for her, but it jolted her to hear this man put it into words.

"He's suffering because word has it you'll be getting married soon."

Wrong again. "He didn't leave much out, did he?" She laughed to cover her distress.

"You have to forgive him. For your information, you're the only person outside my family who knows I'm back after dropping out of sight ten years ago."

"I'm still in shock that you're the missing Causcelle."

"Then you need to eat first to restore yourself." He put the picture on the coffee table and helped her up from the couch. "Now that I've confessed, I'm ready to enjoy our dinner."

A knot of guilt prevented her from moving. "I'm afraid I can't eat until I reveal *my* lie."

That caught his full attention. By the way his hand tightened on her arm, she knew she'd surprised him. His eyes searched hers for an answer.

"Since you've told me the truth about yourself, Jean-Louis, I can do no less because I've been living a lie too. Three weeks ago, I found out my famous father and mother weren't my birth parents after all. Their genes aren't mine. Now *you* have the distinction of being the only person alive who knows that fact aside from the PI I hired to get at the truth and couldn't."

Jean-Louis's heart missed a couple of beats while he absorbed that information before he helped Françoise to the dining room table. "While we enjoy the *saumon en papillotte*, I'd like to hear your story first. Then I'll tell you about mine and the PI my brothers hired to find me, if you're interested." He sat across from her and poured their wine. "What's your real name?"

"Françoise Valmy. I was never given another name." She eyed him curiously. "Why Robert Martin?"

"There are millions of Roberts and Martins in France. I needed to get lost in the shuffle, but we're talking about you." He took a sip of wine. "What happened three weeks ago that turned your life inside out?"

"That's exactly what it did." He watched her eat before she rested her fork on the plate. For the next few minutes, she told him about her father's medical bag and the discovery.

"They never told me I was adopted. That paper lay hidden in the bottom of his bag for twenty-eight years. If it hadn't fallen upside down, I would never have seen it. Maman told me she had three miscarriages before they had me. Of course, I wouldn't have cared about being adopted. What I don't understand was the secrecy. Finding it has left me with too many unsettling questions."

He sat back in the chair, studying her intently. "Considering the caliber of your doctor father, who represented France in Morocco, are you afraid he might have had an affair with a patient before or after he was married? Are you frightened his reputation would be forever tarnished if it came out?"

The man had seized on one of her fears. "Yes. What if he had delivered me, or done something unethical?"

He finished his food. "Maybe he had a lover who couldn't take care of the baby, and he felt responsible because you were his child?"

"You really do know how to ask the right questions. I've thought of that possibility too. Is my birth mother still alive out there somewhere? That's what is killing me. Maybe he was investigated for breaking the rules of the Hippocratic Oath. My father was an attractive man, and there would have been opportunities. He married my mother, who was a beautiful nurse."

"I can believe that," he said under his breath, but she heard him.

"The problem is, I know my parents loved each other. So, if that's true, then it's possible he could have delivered the baby and secretly put it up for adoption before he married. Then he could have talked Maman into going to an adoption agency and they adopted me. I'll never know if she knew or not. I've been lying awake nights wondering about that."

He poured more wine. "Then again, he might have been protecting his patient who'd had an affair with another man. Maybe the father was a government official who couldn't bear exposure at any cost. Or, the woman might have been underage, had a boyfriend and was afraid her parents might find out?"

"The possibilities are endless, Jean-Louis. But perhaps their reason for not telling me had more to do with me. Because I'm a doctor, I can't help but wonder what fatal illness I could have inherited.

"Or is there something in my future like a psychiatric disorder that my parents didn't want me to know about? Will I grow up to be unstable? What did my parents know when they adopted me?

"All this time I thought this omission had to do with some action of my father. But what if they wanted to hide something about my mental or physical condition? These questions are torturing me and make my life uncertain."

Jean-Louis sat forward. "You say this Guillaume Briand from Nice claimed the case was specially sealed under the law."

She nodded. "He said it was done that way because the highest discretion had been necessary. At that point he assured me he couldn't do any more investigating for me and wouldn't take money."

"The man was right. I'm not saying he wasn't good, but it takes someone with years of savvy and certain political connections to get a document like that unsealed. It would be wrong to assume anything yet. What you need is a different kind of expert."

Her eyes narrowed. "Like a man who can get secret and private permission through the help of the president of France himself for example?"

He sensed she wasn't joking. Neither was he. "Maybe."

"That takes more money than I could make in a lifetime. I'm going to have to live with it."

He shook his head. "Knowing you're the best epidemiologist around, you'll never rest until you have answers. But for now, everything you're worrying about is sheer speculation with no basis in truth."

"I realize that, but it has changed my life."

Françoise took another drink of wine. "You're a good listener and I've told you too much. Thank you. Now it's your turn. I want to know why you wanted to drop off the face of the earth for ten years, but I'd love to know the story about this *palais* first. Over the years I've been by this place and the Causcelle Corporation many times, yet I never understood about it since the public wasn't allowed in here."

He lowered his wineglass. "This palace was purchased when my great-great-grandfather bought the other palace to set up Causcelle headquarters a block away. He wanted all the family close by, so this became the family home in Paris complete with a fully staffed kitchen. This suite has always been mine and was still waiting for me after ten years."

"Does it feel good being here again?"

"*Good* isn't exactly the right word. My brothers also had suites while we all went to business school here. But it wasn't home, and contrary to my father's dream for us, I didn't want to go into business. My grades suffered. We had many arguments before I told him I was leaving. Before he could stop me, I joined the army, which I did for many reasons. I made certain he couldn't find me."

There was that pain in his eyes again. "You really did want to get away, didn't you?"

"You'll never know how much. Just now you asked me why I wanted to drop off the face of the earth for ten years. It's interesting you would use those exact words." A low sigh escaped his lips. "How to sum up my twenty-nine years in a few minutes. That's a real challenge. Maybe what I have to show you will help you understand some of my reasons more than anything else could."

He pulled his phone out of his pocket and opened it to his messages. After he'd scrolled to the next text he wanted, he handed his phone to her. "Take a look at that article from

Paris Now. It came out in May of this year. When I first asked my brother Nic what was going on in his life, he told me to read this and he sent it to my phone. I believe you'll find some of the answers to your question."

Beyond curious, Françoise picked it up and started to read.

New Love for one of the Bachelor Billionaire Triplets? For the second time in two years, gorgeous, hunky billionaire Nicolas Causcelle is off the market! All female hopefuls will have to look elsewhere now.

Insider sources report that his former fiancée, Denise Fournette, is "devastated" that Causcelle has found love again so soon after brutally casting her off. Sadly. she didn't have the financial means to make the grade for a Causcelle.

His new lover is reputed to be media-shy Anelise Lavigny, only child and daughter of multimillionaire Hugo Lavigny. In this case it took money to capture money.

Mademoiselle Lavigny was said to be

"inconsolable" after losing her engineer fiancé, Andre Navarre, in a car crash only nineteen months ago, but this liaison between two of France's biggest commercial dynasties seems to have soothed her pain.

Who says money doesn't talk?

The Causcelle triplets have long been the target of scheming mamas. Although, since one of them appears to have disappeared off the face of the earth, that leaves only two delicious men to snap up.

Françoise shuddered when she realized what she'd just asked Jean-Louis.

Good luck, Mademoiselle Lavigny. One has to wonder if the golden boy has staying power this time, or if he'll cast you away in the end.

After reading it twice, Françoise was so sickened she got up from the table and walked back into the living room still clutching his phone. She felt his presence behind her.

"I take it you've figured things out to a certain degree."

She turned around slowly to face him, and handed him back his phone, unable to articulate her feelings.

"What you read only explains part of the agony our family has always faced. The intrusion of the press will never stop being unbearable, but it was my own inner turmoil at nineteen that caused me to run and not look back.

"I couldn't bear the guilt of our family having so much money. Not when there were millions of people in the world who didn't know where their next meal would be coming from. I don't need to tell you what I saw in Africa."

His explanation had reached her soul and helped her understand that wounded look she'd sensed when she'd first met him. "I'm so sorry."

"Not as sorry as I am for behaving like a selfish wretch and walking out on my father. I was the third triplet to be born and didn't have what it took to look life squarely in the eyes like my brothers did. To make my anguish worse, I'd just lost my best friend, Alain, of ten years. When I entered the hospital in Nice, I believed I was dying and I wanted to. It was the coward's way out."

"Not cowardly, Jean-Louis," she rushed to make him feel better. "Anyone wanting to die has to be in a kind of pain that surpasses human understanding."

"You have a remarkable way of putting things, Françoise. I'm afraid Dr. Marouche doesn't have the same bedside manner. To my complete and utter shock, he bluntly said in a loud voice, *You're not dying!*"

"You sounded just like him." It made her laugh.

"My first instinct was to tell him to go to hell because he didn't know what he was talking about."

"It's a good thing you didn't do that."

"I felt too ill to take him on, but I couldn't believe it. I wanted it all to be over so I'd never have to face what a miserable excuse I'd been for a human being. Then you walked in my room and verified what Dr. Marouche had told me. I wanted to hate you, but I couldn't when you were only doing your job and had shown me a lot of understanding."

She could hardly breathe from the remorse and regret pouring out of him.

More than ever, she understood when he'd told her he'd needed to get this off his chest.

"My next shock came when there was a knock on my hotel room door and I discovered my brothers standing there. They'd been looking for me and had finally found me. I felt more shame because they'd had to search the earth for me. Worse, they told me my father was dying. If I wanted to see him before it was too late, I needed to leave with them right then."

"Oh, no—" Françoise wanted to comfort him, but didn't know how and didn't feel she had the right. "How bad is he?"

"Bad."

"That explains why you didn't go in for your next phlebotomy."

"I took care of it at the hospital where my family lives. We live in eastern France outside a little town called La Racineuse."

"Thank heaven you didn't put it off. That's what is making you well. I realize you wouldn't have told me this much and asked me for dinner if you hadn't gone with them."

He nodded. "The Prodigal Son returned and I made my peace with him. With *all* of my family. To my joy, my father is still alive. It's a long story I won't bore you with now."

A soft moan escaped her lips. "I'm so happy

for you about everything, Jean-Louis. More than that, I want to thank you for this evening and for listening to me. I've needed someone to talk to about my problem too. It helps to be able to share the burden with someone we trust. Now I'm afraid I have to go." She was enjoying this way, way too much.

"Are you in a hurry?"

"I want to get an early night. In the morning I'm driving to Bouzy-la-Forêt to visit my great-aunt for the day. She's suffering from emphysema. I promised I'd visit her after taking my boards and want to show her my new car. It'll be fun to try out the Nissan."

"Does she have family with her?"

"No. Her husband died four years ago and they couldn't have children."

"Then you must be a great comfort to her."

"I hope so. I also have to admit to another objective. Now that my parents and grand-parents have passed, she's the only person alive who could possibly tell me about my adoption. That is *if* she ever knew about it. But they might have sworn her to secrecy. She and Maman were very close. Still, I have hope that she'll understand my pain and tell me what she knows, *if* she knows something."

His compassionate smile filled her with warmth. "I knew you'd go on digging. It's in your nature."

"You're right. So, tell me. Are you flying back home?"

"In a day or two after I've done some more research."

She rolled her eyes. "You've left out the details, but that sounds interesting."

He cocked his head. "It could be. How about I tag along with you tomorrow and I'll tell you about it? Bouzy is as good a place as any to start on a project I've been planning. While you visit your great-aunt, I'll do some searching in and around the village. For what it's worth, I'm a good mechanic. If anything should happen to your car en route, I can repair it."

"Are you serious?" The thought of spending a day with him made her dizzy with excitement. She was out of her mind.

"Ask the army. Alain and I got ourselves out of many a fix."

How terrible he'd lost his friend. "If you really want to, of course you can come with me. I'd planned to leave town by seven thirty."

"Whenever, wherever you say."

"Why don't I pick you up at the entrance."

"I'll be ready."

"You don't mind a woman driver?" she teased.

"Women make some of the best drivers. I found that out after I joined the military."

Before she knew it, Jean-Louis had walked her out to the elevator and they descended to the main floor. When they'd come here earlier, she'd had no idea what to expect. All she knew was that in the sharing of their stories, she'd felt a connection that had made them friends.

Jean-Louis walked her to her car. "Maybe the visit tomorrow will settle all your fears."

"Certainly Monsieur Briand couldn't give me any hope."

"I didn't think I had hope either until you found a cure for me. That was a miraculous moment in time. I've discovered that I like being alive and human." His comment reminded her of her dream about him. "It's long past time I started to redeem myself. Thank you for having dinner with me."

"The pleasure was all mine, believe me." Jean-Louis could never know what it meant to her.

He shut the door and she drove away while she thought about what he'd said. *Redeem himself.*

Françoise still didn't know which part of his story brought him the most pain. He'd been one of the walking wounded that had taken him on a long ten-year journey. But he seemed to be recovering. As for her pain, it had started three weeks ago and she had the terrifying thought it would never end.

CHAPTER FOUR

SUNDAY MORNING, Jean-Louis had been chatting with Guy for twenty minutes when the sight of the metallic blue car pulling up to the *palais* entrance suddenly quickened his pulse.

"That's one beautiful female, Jean-Louis."

He'd found that out the day before yesterday when he'd seen her for the first time without her mask. It had struck him then that she had to be the most gorgeous woman he'd ever met in his life.

"I agree. See you later."

When he climbed in the car outside, he couldn't help but notice her neck-length black-brown hair that framed a perfect oval face. "You've chosen a beautiful day for a drive, Françoise."

"We're lucky. It shouldn't take us more than two hours to reach Bouzy."

"It took my brothers and I a little longer on our bikes years ago."

"I'll bet." She chuckled before driving them out to the street.

Beneath those finely arched dark brows glowed the lustrous green eyes with dark lashes he'd remembered in his hospital room. As for her mouth, its natural curvature would drive any man wild with desire to taste it. He thought of the man intending to be her future husband. Jean-Louis understood Antoine's dilemma.

"Does your great-aunt know you're coming?"

"No. I want to surprise her. Thank you for being on time. Have you eaten?"

"Not yet." He was starving.

"I haven't either. There's a café called L'Auberge I like in Bouzy. They serve the most scrumptious, creamy scrambled eggs on toasted baguette slices you've ever tasted. Their hot chocolate with *crème fleurette de Normandie* is to die for."

"I used to dream about food like that after my company had been out of rations close to a week."

She made a groaning sound and he laughed.

Before long they'd joined the A-6 going south. "Where were you and your brothers headed during that bike ride?"

"We wanted to explore the Loiret area and see the bawdy wooden friezes at Bellegarde castle."

"Guys." She shook her head.

"Yup. We can be kind of awful."

"I would have loved a brother. Do you have sisters? I only remember that you were triplet brothers."

"We have three."

"How glorious! Six children."

"Four spouses and five nieces and nephews. It's been fun being with everyone again after a decade."

"I envy you your large family." She darted him a glance. "You said you'd tell me about this project of yours. What is this research you're doing? I'd love to hear about it."

Françoise showed an interest that made her fun to talk to. "First, I need to explain that from the beginning I had decided to become a career officer. When I met Alain, he thought that's what he would do too."

"You had to have undergone an incredible

change the moment you entered the military, yet you adapted to it over all those years."

"We didn't have a choice. During that time, we saw soldiers being discharged because of one problem or another. Many of them had joined at a young age and didn't have the schooling or means to thrive back in society. I spent those years wondering how to help them. Some vets with all kinds of wounds and injuries were released with little hope and nothing to look forward to."

She nodded. "I've taken care of some of them."

"Of course you have. Well, it wasn't until Alain died that I decided to leave the service and put my ideas into action. But by then I began to feel so ill, I was certain I didn't have long to live and was discharged. You know the rest. When I realized I wasn't going to die, I used those two weeks in the hospital to put real substance to my ideas."

"I could never have guessed what was going on inside that brain of yours."

A half smile broke out on his mouth. "When you told me I didn't have to stay at the hospital anymore, I couldn't wait to get started. I made dozens of phone calls to the veterans' division of the army to trace returning veterans and ask them to get in touch with me. That's when my brothers found me."

"And to Antoine's alarm, you took off. Please go on. You have me riveted."

"Everything in my family has changed because my father is dying. My brothers no longer work or live in Paris like they once did. When I flew back here a few days ago, I walked around the empty *palais* and thought what a waste. It contains twelve suites like mine, a staff kitchen that makes all the meals, maids, housekeeping, security. But for what at this point?

"When I fly home in a few days, I plan to ask my father and family how they would feel if the *palais* could be used for a real purpose. It's asking a lot, but—"

"But worth a try," she interrupted, "for an amazingly worthy cause. So many returning vets need help."

"Yes! If they could have housing and go to school to learn a trade, it would make a difference in a few lives. What I'd like to do is set up a fund to aid them in going to school here in Paris. They could live free at the *palais*."

"How fantastic would that be!"

"I agree. When they've achieved enough schooling, I'd arrange for different businesses around France to hire them. Some could be nurses, armed guards, firefighters, parole officers, substance abuse counselors, computer operators." He angled his head toward her. "What do you think?"

She was quiet for a minute. "You *have* to know the answer to that question." Her voice trembled. "Your desire to do good knows no bounds. The world needs more men like you."

"You mean a guy who left his family for ten years when they needed him?"

"Stop belittling yourself," she scolded. "You know what I mean. We've arrived in Bouzy, Jean-Louis. Breakfast will be my treat."

Françoise drove into the quaint village and parked in front of the family-owned L'Auberge. They went inside to eat breakfast. Later, over a second cup of cocoa, he said, "Why don't you leave me here? I'll walk around the village and start doing my research. Let's trade phone numbers to stay in touch. When you're ready to go back to Paris, call me."

Françoise pulled the phone from her purse. With that accomplished, she got to her feet.

"Stay there and enjoy yourself." She put some euros on the table. "Expect a call from me this afternoon when I'm ready to leave Silver Pines."

He nodded. "I think I'll start my quest right here with the man over at the counter. I'll feel him out about hiring a vet who's been a cook and has credentials from a cooking school."

She smiled. "Knowing you, I'm convinced anything is possible. Go for it."

"Thanks for the encouragement."

Within ten minutes she reached the rest home and spoke with Thea, a daytime nurse who took care of the residents. Françoise loved her. "How is Nadine doing? I'd like to take her outside."

Thea shook her head. "I'm sorry, but she's not well. Almost overnight she developed bronchitis and needs oxygen. The doctor came in to check on her last night. You'll see on his notes that her dementia has grown worse. She only says a few words now. I'm sorry. If you need anything, ring the desk."

"Of course. Thank you for all you do for her."

With a heavy heart she walked to the room and leaned over her eighty-five-year-old great-aunt. There'd be no going anywhere with her, the poor darling. She lay under the covers looking exhausted each time she coughed. Tears filled Françoise's eyes.

"Mame?" She whispered her pet name for her after kissing her forehead.

The older woman made a sound. "Dionne?"

The doctor was right. Nadine's dementia had grown worse since the last visit. "No. It's Françoise."

She coughed again. "Who?"

"Dionne's daughter," Françoise answered.

"I wanted one."

"I know."

She muttered something about Albert, her deceased husband.

Françoise leaned closer. "What did Albert say, Mame?"

After another coughing spasm Françoise heard, "No adoption."

Her stomach clenched. Was that proof that Nadine knew something? Or did she mean her husband hadn't wanted to adopt a child? She sat down on a chair at the side of the bed. Her great-aunt didn't want to talk and Françoise wouldn't dream of wearing her out. There'd be no answers here.

She stayed with her until a few minutes after three. During those hours against a background of more coughing spells, Françoise told her about her life now. She explained how she'd met one of the famous Causcelle triplets. Françoise talked about taking her boards and that she was now working in the hospital in Paris where her father had worked.

Only when she told her that she'd broken it off with Eric Moreau did the older woman make a sound. "Sad…" she murmured.

"It's for the best, Mame."

"No baby…"

The words broke Françoise's heart. Nadine had suffered because she hadn't been able to have children. Neither had Françoise's mother. Her mind was in a different place.

After giving her a final kiss, she left the room and asked the staff and Thea to keep her posted no matter the hour. Françoise was responsible for her. After phoning Jean-Louis, who would wait for her at the petrol station on the north end of the village, she left the rest home with a whole new heartache.

Bouzy was too far away from Paris for Françoise to visit every day. Maybe she could find a position at a hospital in a town closer to here, so she could make daily visits. Even though her mind was still deep in thought when she reached Jean-Louis, she couldn't help but notice him because he stood out. Not because of his tan suit and white shirt his build did wonders for. It was the man himself.

What had the newspaper said?

Gorgeous, hunky billionaire Nicolas Causcelle is off the market! All female hopefuls will have to look elsewhere now.

Those words described all three brothers. If Françoise needed proof, she only had to recall Celestine's reaction to meeting Jean-Louis at the desk at the hospital. It had reminded her of his female visitor's similar reaction at the hospital in Nice. Her face and eyes had worn the same infatuated expression.

He's the hunkiest man I ever saw in my life and he's a vet! I didn't know there were men like him in existence!

No, Françoise thought to herself as she drew closer to him. There weren't, not like the inside or the outside of that particular male.

She pulled to a stop so he could climb in.

After he buckled up, she looked at him. "How was your day?"

"Successful in several ways. How about yours?"

Françoise started the car and drove toward the main street leading out of the village toward Paris. She told him about Nadine and her bronchitis. "I don't know how much longer she'll live."

"I'm sorry, Françoise."

"So am I. She didn't recognize me. She thought I was my mother."

"Poor thing. I take it she couldn't shed any light on the adoption paper you found."

She told him what her great-aunt had said. "I don't know. If she did give something away, I'm sure it was by accident. Her comment could have been taken two ways."

"You're right, and I can see you need cheering up. I'll call ahead to Chez Aline, near the Bastille. Have you ever eaten there?"

"No, but I've heard others rave about it."

"I'll order us some Prince de Paris *jambon-beurre baguettes.* It'll be a meal as delicious as our breakfast after our return to the *palais.* My treat this time." He set the address on her GPS.

"I'll be salivating all the way back."

He pulled out his phone and made the call to the restaurant before putting it in his jacket pocket. She felt his gaze on her and sensed something was on his mind.

"Françoise? I know a man who might be able to help you. He's the one my brothers called to find me. I hesitated to say anything before you spoke to your great-aunt, but now I know you could use his services."

"I could never afford them, Jean-Louis."

"It would cost you nothing."

She shook her head. "I appreciate your magnificent offer more than I can say, but I have to refuse. One of the reasons you left France for a decade was to get away from a world that wanted a piece of you. You've shared one of your dreams with me that has revealed the selfless side of your nature. I couldn't let that generosity extend to me."

"Françoise—listen to me. I—"

"I'm not a vet without a home or a career," she cut him off. "I've had the best life with the best parents anyone could ever have. Whatever went on in my father's past, he and my mother showered me with love. While I sat with my great-aunt today, I realized her one dream was to have a child, but that hope never materialized. Yet she endured her trial and led a wonderful life.

"I need to learn from her and endure something that hurts too. I have to find the strength and faith to know my parents kept the adoption a secret because they believed it was right."

"That's a laudable speech, but if you ever change your mind…"

"Thank you, but I won't. For now, I'd like to hear about your successes today."

He put on his sunglasses and turned to her. "Even though it's Sunday, some businesses were open. I talked to managers and owners throughout the day. Do you know that every one of them was willing to consider hiring a vet after I told them my plan?"

Her mouth curved upward. "Even the owner of the café where we had breakfast?"

"He told me they usually hire family because he belongs to a large one, but he'd be willing to give a vet a chance. There's goodness in most everyone. People want to help. Today has proved to me this experience will be repeated wherever I go and gives me hope for my plans."

"That doesn't surprise me."

"I have you to thank for spurring me on, Françoise. I know you think it's because I'm a Causcelle, but I introduced myself as Robert Martin and told them I had formed a company to aid returning vets."

She gripped the wheel harder. "Actually, I didn't think about that at all. But whether you had told me or not, I know it's *you*, Jean-Louis, and your sincerity after serving in the military that spoke to their minds and hearts. I'm so thrilled for you."

"I'm happy for you too."

"What do you mean?"

"Back in Nice I learned about a certain important man in your life."

Françoise gritted her teeth. "That Antoine is a menace."

"You know you don't mean it. He intimated you've been involved with one of the men on the French trade commission to Morocco. Apparently this one is a Moreau, and I know that family happens to live in one of the famous nineteenth-century Auteuil villas in Paris. Antoine said you'll probably be getting married soon and it will be the match of the season."

She took a quick breath. "Antoine got ahead of himself along with all the hospital gossip."

"Am I wrong to be congratulating you yet?"

"I'm afraid so, but it's not your fault. Eric and I were never engaged and we won't be getting married."

Out of the corner of her eye she noticed Jean-Louis's hand suddenly clench on his thigh. Why?

"I guess Antoine isn't in the loop on that piece of news."

"No. But he did notice on your chart you had a visitor after you didn't show up for your next phlebotomy."

"Who?"

"The young woman holding a sack." Was she someone special to him? Françoise got angry with herself for wanting an answer to that question.

"You mean Suzanne, my friend Alain's sister. The day I stepped off the transport plane, I visited his father, who runs a small body shop. I wanted to pay my respects and give his family some photos of their son. He knew I was headed for the hospital. Before I left Nice, I presented Alain's father with a gift from him. She brought me some dessert her mother had made. It was their family's thank-you."

That answered that. "They sound like a lovely family. What was Alain's gift? One of his possessions?"

"In a manner of speaking, yes. It's a Ferrari dealership his son eventually bought and paid for after having given ten years of his life to military service. He died before he could turn it over to his father, so I acted in Alain's place to take care of it."

She was speechless for a moment as she pondered what he'd said. "That's the most wonderful thing I ever heard. Not only his love for his family, but your love for him."

"He took the place of my brothers over those ten years. Every time he talked about his terrific father and mother, I suffered shame over the way I'd treated mine. My father pushed me into business though I'd wanted to be a mechanic on the estate. But that's all in the past. Enough about me. Françoise, I'm truly sorry about you and the man you were involved with. Forgive me for bringing up something painful."

"You didn't!" she blurted. "It was never meant to be. What I'm facing now is the question of my whole life. Think about it, Jean-Louis. When you look in a mirror, you *know* who you are. I envy you that more than you can imagine."

"I'm not inside your skin, but you're still Françoise Valmy to me, epidemiologist extraordinaire. Whether you have your adoptive parents' genes or your birth parents', it has nothing to do with the woman you've become. I, for one, owe you my life. That's all that really matters."

She shook her head. No. That wasn't all that really mattered, but Jean-Louis didn't need to hear more about the agony she'd been going through. "I'll try to maintain a positive attitude." By now they'd reached Paris and she needed to be alone before she broke down.

Within the month she'd like to find work at a hospital where her father hadn't been a fixture. It needed to be in a town near Bouzy so she could visit her great-aunt every day. Nadine was her only family now. She'd get an apartment and settle in to take care of her. It would be a new life.

"Françoise?" A deep male voice broke in on her thoughts. "Keep following the map to the Rue de la Roquette and wait out in front of the café. I'll run in to get our food."

"I can't wait."

CHAPTER FIVE

ANTOINE HAD BEEN a menace after all.

Jean-Louis had assumed he'd been safe around Françoise, a nearly married woman, but the information fed to him in Nice about Moreau hadn't been reliable. This was the exact situation he'd never wanted to happen with any woman. It had been a mistake to drive to Bouzy with her. She'd burrowed so deeply under his skin, he might not be able to get her out. He feared in his gut that he was already beyond the point of no return.

Once he'd picked up their food, Françoise drove them to the *palais* and they ate outside in the car. He couldn't help admiring the way she looked in her yellow two-piece summer suit, like a vision in the sunlight.

"Thank you for this, Jean-Louis. I didn't realize how hungry I was."

"You've just reminded me I haven't thanked you for buying us breakfast."

No woman had ever paid for him before. That was crazy when she'd been the one to save his life. It was his fault that he'd asked if he could come with her today…because…because he had to admit he craved her company. But he feared acknowledging it. To get close to a woman only to lose her terrified him.

As he sat there, Jean-Louis realized he was in serious trouble. He'd thought he was safe until she'd dropped the bomb telling him she wasn't going to marry Moreau and had never been engaged. Once he went inside the *palais*, would he have the willpower never to see her again?

She turned to him. "You were right about these sandwiches. Food for the gods."

"My brothers and I went there often between classes."

"I can see why."

Get out of the car. Make a clean break. Now!

He'd finished the last of his baguette. "Unfortunately, all good things have to end. I can't thank you enough for letting me drive with you today. It was a rare treat with you at the wheel of your new car. I accomplished more than I dreamed."

I've also learned I've been holding a live grenade in my hand.

He opened the door and got out with their empty sacks. She leaned toward him. "I'm so glad you came with me. Take care of yourself and never fail to make an appointment to get your blood drawn."

"Believe me I won't. Try not to worry too much about this mystery in your life. One day you may get answers. Let's hope your great-aunt recovers soon from her bronchitis. *Au revoir*, Françoise."

Once inside the *palais*, Jean-Louis hurried to his suite before he ran back out to stop her from leaving. After he took a shower, he could hear the phone ring and threw on a robe to get it. In his heart of hearts, he hoped it was Françoise who hadn't wanted to say goodbye either. He reached for it on the bedside table. When he saw the caller ID and realized it was coming from his sister Corinne, he grew alarmed. They all worried about their father.

He clicked on. *"Eh, bien, ma soeur. Qu'est-ce qui se passe?"*

"I'm glad you picked up. I'm calling on behalf of Papa. He hasn't stopped brooding about your blood disorder. He feels so guilty for not knowing how you suffered. Dr. Simonesse came by earlier and they got talking. Papa's wondering if the disorder grew inside of him and that's why he has heart failure."

"I've wondered too."

"The doctor is willing to consult with your doctor because Papa would rather your specialist came here to take care of his blood work. But you know Papa. He fears it might be asking too much of you, and he wouldn't blame you if you turned him down. I told him I'd find out. What do you think? Would it be possible?"

The chance of being with Françoise again shouldn't have filled him with this rush of exhilaration. His watch said eight thirty. "I'll do anything for Papa. Let me try to get hold of Dr. Valmy and maybe I'll call you back tonight."

"That would be wonderful. Thanks, *frérot*. I love it that you're home after all these years."

"I love it more." He clicked off and called Françoise without hesitation, but she'd put her phone on call forwarding. After leaving his name, he asked her to phone if she could, no matter how late. It was important. He'd never forget that moment when his loving father had held out his arms to him and forgiven him. The man didn't have his physical strength anymore, but inside him lived the soul of a saint and Jean-Louis would do anything for him.

He was still pacing the floor two hours later when his cell rang. She was calling him back. He grabbed it and sank down on the side of the bed. "Françoise?"

"Jean-Louis—I'm sorry I couldn't call back until now." She sounded a little out of breath. "Are you ill?"

Of course she would ask. She was a doctor. "*Non, non.* I'm sorry if you thought it was urgent. But it *is* important. I know you didn't expect to hear from me. Forgive me for disturbing you."

"That's nonsense. What's wrong?"

He gripped the phone tighter. "This concerns my father." He explained about Corinne's call. "I know Papa, and he's agitating over it."

"Well, we can't have that. I'd be happy to do this for you."

He heard no hesitation in her voice. She couldn't know what this meant to him. But since she was a doctor, he didn't dare read more into it beyond her need to be of help. "The whole family thanks you."

"No problem, but your father's doctor will have to contact my boss, Dr. Soulis. Let me talk to him tomorrow and I'll get back to you. If he says yes, then we'll make the arrangements and I'll plan to take some time off from the hospital. I realize your father can't travel."

"You're a saint."

"Hardly that."

Something in her tone worried him. "Françoise? Are you all right? You don't quite sound yourself."

"I'm not. You're very perceptive. Eric was waiting for me when I got back to my apartment. That's why I couldn't call you right away."

He took a quick breath. "I see."

"It's good he has to go back to Morocco in a few days."

Jean-Louis smothered a moan. The sooner the better. "Try to get some sleep if you can. We'll talk later."

The second they hung up, he phoned Corinne and told her it would probably work out fine. He'd call her tomorrow with details.

When he clicked off, he fell back on the bed thinking about being with Françoise again, this time on his home turf.

His feelings for her dominated everything, including any thoughts of self-preservation. After years of avoiding entanglements, it was finally happening.

But he couldn't afford to forget.

An entanglement took two.

"Entrez!"

Françoise opened the door to Dr. Soulis's office Monday morning. "Can we talk for a few minutes when you're not busy?"

"I'm all yours. Come in and sit down." He studied her. "Are you all right?"

"I'm not sure. You were so wonderful to consider hiring me, and now I find myself in a real dilemma I couldn't have imagined before today."

"What's wrong?"

"Two things. First, I need your permission to leave work for a day to attend to a man dying of heart failure. You'll recognize the name Louis Causcelle."

His eyes widened. "Who doesn't know about

the most famous entrepreneur of his generation? How are you associated with him?"

She cleared her throat. "His son was a patient of mine in Nice for two weeks." Françoise went on to explain everything to him. "His doctor will phone you to ask permission for me to fly to eastern France and draw his blood."

Christophe smiled. "In a heartbeat."

"Thank you, but that's not all. This is about my great-aunt." She told him everything, including her desire to live near her. But a move would mean giving up this coveted position with him.

"Say no more, Françoise. As you know, my widower father is very ill and depends on me and my wife for everything. You're her only relative and she needs you as much as you need her. Since you haven't even worked here a week, why don't you take a week's vacation now to look into everything and arrange for some interviews. As for Louis Causcelle, I'll tell his doctor you have my permission to draw his blood. That shouldn't take too long out of one day."

Tears fell down her cheeks. "I don't know how to begin to thank you. I feel so honored to be working here with you, but I just need to sort things out first."

He sat back. "I'm glad this has happened now. You can't do your work if you're worried about your only loved one. If you do move from Paris to work at a different hospital near her, I won't be happy about it, but I'll totally understand. You're free to leave now. I'll see you in a week."

Françoise had been wrong. Jean-Louis wasn't the only male on the planet with exceptional goodness coursing through his veins. Christophe was right up there too.

On Tuesday morning at eight thirty Françoise walked out of her apartment building with her overnight bag to wait for Jean-Louis under a partially cloudy sky. He'd called earlier for her address and told her not to eat breakfast. They'd have a meal on the jet.

Yesterday Dr. Soulis had talked with Louis's doctor and encouraged Françoise to do whatever she could to satisfy the ailing older man's questions.

Since learning that Jean-Louis was a Causcelle, Françoise had a natural curiosity about their whole family and had to admit she was looking forward to this visit with more anticipation than was warranted. Jean-Louis had everything to do with it. Besides his background, she'd never met a more complicated, fascinating man in her life.

She found it ironic that the door to a new life had just opened for him. Yet another door had slammed shut on her, crushing her dreams for a normal, fulfilling future.

While Françoise stood watching for his black Mercedes, he came for her in a white limo. Her heart raced faster as he got out to help her in with her case. This time he'd arrived in a dark blue suit with white shirt and tie. In trying to describe his dark male beauty, she'd run out of superlatives.

He sat down next to her and the limo drove off. "I like that dress you're wearing." Their gazes met. "The color matches your eyes. You would never know you're the same masked doctor from the hospital in Nice."

"You don't resemble the sick vet lying in that hospital bed either."

They both smiled before he said, "There aren't enough ways to say thank you for doing this. It's asking a lot."

"No need for more thanks. I'm a doctor and am as curious as you to see if there's any connection between your father's condition and yours."

"Then I hope you won't mind if I ask you another favor while we're there."

She never knew what he was going to say next. That's what made him so intriguing. "Why would I mind?"

"It's about my brothers. Since we're identical triplets, I—"

"You're worried they might have your disorder too?" Françoise broke in while she studied his arresting profile. "Have they been showing symptoms too?"

"If so, they've said nothing to me, but I'll tell you more after we're in the air."

They'd reached the small airport where a sparkling white jet with the Causcelle name and logo stood on the tarmac. Jean-Louis pulled her overnight bag from the back seat and helped her on board. They sat in the lounge compartment and strapped themselves in. Before long they taxied out to the runway and took off. Being with him made everything they did an unprecedented experience for her.

When they'd gained altitude, they undid their seat belts. The steward, on friendly terms with Jean-Louis, served them a meal of quiche Lorraine and wine, which she thoroughly enjoyed. "That tasted delicious." She wiped her mouth with a napkin. "I've never flown in a private jet. This is wonderful."

He nodded. "It beats the transport plane that brought me into Nice."

On that flight he'd believed he was returning to France to die. She wanted to change the subject. "Tell me more about the concern for your brothers."

Jean-Louis turned to her. "At the hospital, when you asked me if I had any males in my family showing symptoms, I lied to you, which I'm sorry for. But you got me thinking. When I reconciled with Papa and told him the reason for my discharge, I'm afraid it got him thinking and he's been worried about it ever since. He wants my brothers tested along with himself."

"After learning what's wrong with you, of course he's anxious. Do they know I'm coming?"

"Yes, but not to test them. The problem is, Nic and Raoul are as stoic about themselves and what goes on with them as I am. If they've ever had any of my symptoms, they never told our father. But now they're going to have to for the sake of their health."

"Will they cooperate?"

"If my brothers resist, my father will urge them to get tested in such a way they won't be able to say no."

It sounded like Louis Causcelle was the source of the irresistible force Jean-Louis had inherited. "I'll make it as painless as possible. To keep things simple, let me run a basic blood test on them and your father immediately. If I don't find any abnormalities, then there'll be no need to put them through the tests you had to undergo and your worries will be over."

"And you'll conclude I was the only abnormal child in the Causcelle household."

"Correct. There's usually one of those in every family."

His chuckle tickled her. "We'll be landing at Chalon Champforgeuil airport in a minute. From there we'll drive to the château."

"What's it like?"

"The original building was deeded to the family in the twelve hundreds by Philip II. There've been dozens of renovations since. My sister Corinne and her husband live there with her family to help take care of our father and his health caregiver, Luca. Raoul lives there now as does Nic with his wife, Anelise. They occupy another part of the château.

"They're building a home on the estate and will be moving out of the château in another month or two. My other sisters and their families live on our grounds too. Everyone comes in and out. But don't worry. There's a guest room waiting for you at the château."

The Causcelle family lived larger than life. No doubt there were many guest rooms. "I imagine it's a big estate."

"Yes, with everything you can think of, including the fromagerie, grange, a hothouse, gardens, orchards, farms, barns, a dairy, outbuildings, storage sheds, pastures, cattle, sheep, corrals. The list goes on and on."

She angled her head toward him. "Why didn't you mention a garage? You told me you used to work in it after school and that's why you felt so tired. Does it still exist?"

He smiled. "You never forget anything, do you? Yes, it's as pathetic as ever."

"That's because you've been away ten years. Now that you're back, I presume you have plans for it."

"We'll see."

"Have you spent time in it since returning from Africa?"

His eyes searched hers. "I would have liked to. You know too many of my secrets already."

"Well, I know you were a captain in the army, but I'm positive they gave you a mechanic's job in the beginning."

"Alain and I got assigned to work on machinery."

She smiled. "A match made for two guys who liked using their hands while your genius brains figured out what was wrong."

The jet lounge resounded with Jean-Louis's laughter.

"You *are* geniuses, Jean-Louis. My father used to say that creating a world required an engineer/mechanic to start the whole process. The engineer would figure out what was needed and the mechanic would start fixing it."

Jean-Louis grinned at her. "Your father left himself out."

"When I said that to him, he shook his head. 'My darling daughter, God was *the* great engineer/mechanic and healer. Everything else came after.' When I thought about it, I knew he was right."

"*You* are a healer, Françoise, in more ways than you know. I'm curious to see what secrets you discover after drawing our blood."

"So am I. Maybe I'll find the genius gene that set your family apart from the beginning. But I'll keep it a secret. Otherwise, it will give the world another excuse to invade your privacy."

He sent her an intense glance. "You really do understand, don't you?" Just then the Fasten Seat Belts light flashed. They were about to land in the world Jean-Louis had been born to. She'd never been so eager for anything in her life.

The conversation with Françoise had sent new thrills through him. His euphoria stayed with him as he found one of the estate cars at the small airport to drive them to La Racineuse.

When they passed the town sign, she turned to him. "I know *racine* means root— your high school logo. What does *racineuse* mean?"

"As you know, the *euse* part means doer. Put it on the end of *racine* and around here the word has come to mean a man who is tenacious, stubborn and a doer."

The car filled with her laughter. "It goes right along with everything you told me about your father."

He sent her an answering smile. "Papa is the biggest tenacious, stubborn doer of this century. Do you think when you draw his blood, you'll be able to identify that particular stubborn gene? Will it show up in Raoul or Nic?"

"That's a question I've never even thought about. You've just suggested a whole new field of research for me."

"Your mind never stops working. As long as we're nearing the town, we'll swing by the hospital first. That way you can get what you need and be able to draw Papa's blood after we reach the château today."

"You're making this so easy for me."

"That's because you're going out of your way for our family. He's afraid he might die before he finds out if he has PV. As you know, he blames himself for not having known what was wrong with me. I told him it was my fault for never mentioning my symptoms, but he can't get over it."

"The poor darling. While at the hospital here, I'll get what I need to take your brothers' blood too. Then they won't have to make a trip unless it becomes necessary."

"Thank you for being so thoughtful and generous, Françoise. How was I lucky enough to end up with you as my doctor in Nice? I still marvel."

"You can stop thanking me. I'm still amazed that I met *you*." She cocked her head. "Jean-Louis? Do you know how rare it is for the mother's egg to split into three? And that all three of you were born identical and healthy? Your blood disorder doesn't count."

His brows lifted. "One in ten thousand?"

"That's with the help of fertility drugs. Did your mom use them?"

"No. My parents already had three girls. They decided to try one more time for a boy, but they had little hope."

She laughed again. "Without those drugs, you're looking at a case of one set of triplets in *one million*!"

"You're joking—"

"*Non*. You Causcelle triplets have defied the odds. With your permission, I'd like to write it up for the medical journal. The press won't see it, but doctors around the world will love it."

"I'll think about it." But he doubted he could ever deny her anything. On he drove until they reached the hospital, where he pulled up in the front parking area.

"Is this the place where history was made?" she cried.

He turned off the engine and smiled at her. "You mean where an emergency room doctor sewed up my hand when the air hammer jammed a chisel bit into it? *That* made history."

"I'll bet it did when you were supposed to be in bed."

"You're right. The ambulance came to the garage at midnight to cart me away. I had a biology test at school the next day and failed it miserably by mixing up paramecium and protozoa. Needless to say, my father was not a happy man."

More chuckling rippled out of her. "That sounds pretty traumatic, but it still doesn't match your sensational birth. I liked that high school photo of the three of you, but I have to admit I'm eager to see all of you together in person. It'll be a privilege."

Being with Françoise made him thankful to be alive. He jumped out of the car and they went inside. "The lab is on the second floor, west end."

The doctor on duty had been alerted they were coming and helped her gather the items she'd need. Before long they left the building and drove to the château.

When his home came into view, Jean-Louis heard her slight cry of wonder. The unexpected sight of it in the distance always affected visitors that way. After being gone ten years, seeing it again that first day and all it represented had been so overwhelming, the guys had left him alone in the car for a little while to deal with his emotions.

"Oh—" Her gorgeous face had lit up. "You just don't expect to see a glorious château in the distance that looks like it should be in Paris."

Jean-Louis agreed about the glorious sight, but at the moment his whole attention was focused on the breathtaking woman who'd infiltrated his every thought.

He drove to the front area of the château, facing one of the rose gardens, and pulled her bag and hospital case from the car. Together they entered the foyer. "Your room is upstairs where you can freshen up. Then I'll take you to meet my father."

Dozens of framed family pictures decorated the walls as they climbed the stairs. Françoise would love to have time to look at all of them. An attractive brunette was just coming out of the bedroom on the second floor.

"Jean-Louis! I didn't know you'd arrived. I wanted to make sure there were fresh towels in here."

Françoise watched him give her a hug. "Corinne? Meet Dr. Valmy, the epidemiologist who diagnosed my problem. Françoise? This is my sister Corinne, who's taking wonderful care of Papa."

To think their mother had died before she could finish raising her daughters or hold her baby boys. How terrible that Jean-Louis and his siblings had lost their incredible *maman* that night, and so tragic for their father, who'd lost his wife.

"It's a pleasure to meet you, Corinne." They shook hands. "I don't want to cause you any inconvenience."

She shook her head. "We're all ecstatic

you're here. You've not only saved our brother's life, you've brought new hope to our father, who never thought to see Jean-Louis again. I honestly believe he's looking better today."

Her words touched Françoise. "That's remarkable news."

"I'll join you downstairs and we'll visit Papa in his bedroom. He knows you were coming to draw blood so he agreed to stay in bed." She walked away.

"He doesn't sound too *racineuse* to me," Françoise whispered to Jean-Louis. His black gaze fused with hers. The shared moment remembering their conversation in the car set her vital organ fibrillating. Who had the heart problem right now?

Jean-Louis carried her things into the bedroom. "You go ahead and freshen up, Françoise. My bedroom is two doors down the hall. I'll meet you in the salon on the right of the foyer. Take all the time you need."

"I won't be long." She closed the door and looked around. Seeing his magnificent home made her wonder how he could have left for ten years, except that she *did* understand the reasons.

After opening the lab kit, she washed her hands in the en suite bathroom and pulled out a wrapped packet of surgical gloves. Once she'd put on a surgical mask, she picked up the kit and left to go downstairs, anxious to meet the dynamo of the Causcelle Corporation.

Finding herself alone, she wandered over to the portrait above the hearth. The beautiful raven-haired woman had bequeathed parts of herself to Jean-Louis and his sister. A special spot in Françoise's soul ached for the woman who'd died before she got to know all her wonderful children. It hurt her to realize Jean-Louis had never known his mother. Francesca had never known her birth mother either. That was something they had in common.

"Papa had this hung after my brothers and I were born." Jean-Louis had just come in the room. "He said he wanted our mother to be front and center so we'd never forget."

"As if you could. What was her name?"

"Delphine Ronfleur."

How wonderful that Jean-Louis could look at that painting and know it was his mother.

Clearly, Louis Causcelle had loved his wife.

That was the kind of love Françoise had always wanted. But unexpected circumstances had altered the course of her once-dreamed-of future. As she'd told Eric, *I'm not sure I'll ever get married.*

She turned to Jean-Louis. "Your mother is so lovely."

"I think so too," but he was staring at Françoise. "I can see you're ready. It's a shame you're wearing your mask. Papa won't be able to see all of you, and he won't like it."

"That's not important."

"I couldn't disagree more." Everything he said in that deep voice made her tremble. "Let's go."

They went back out to the foyer and walked down a hall. Corinne and the health caregiver she introduced as Luca met them in front of a set of double doors. They were opened into a veritable apartment with its own sitting room.

"Papa?" she called out. "We're coming in."

The four of them entered the bedroom. By its appointments, Françoise could imagine a duke or a count living in here once upon a time. Her gaze flew to the balding man sitting against pillows, his long body under the covers.

At a glance she could see he'd given his sons their striking bone structure and height. When he'd had hair, he would have been a very handsome man. Right now, his color looked surprisingly good for a patient in this stage of heart failure.

He studied Françoise out of dark eyes. "Please pull down your mask for a few seconds, Dr. Valmy. I want to see the face of the woman who saved my son's life."

The source of the irresistible force had spoken. She did his bidding, then put it back in place. Out of the corner of her eye she could tell Jean-Louis was trying hard not to smile.

"It's a good thing you have to wear one around your male patients," he kept talking. "A woman who looks like you needs all the protection she can get. I appreciate your dropping everything to come here so quickly. I'm anxious to know if this PV has invaded the whole male side of my family."

"We'll find out very soon, Monsieur Causcelle."

"Please call me Louis."

"If you'll call me Françoise."

"Done." The older man smiled.

Jean-Louis put one of the chairs next to the

bed, where she sat down and reached in the kit for the stethoscope. "Let me just check you out first. By the way, Louis, I like your blue silk pajamas."

"My grandchildren gave them to me."

"They have excellent taste. All right. Just breathe in and hold it."

She took her time listening to his chest and back. When she'd finished, she said, "I think you're a fraud. You sound much better than I thought you would. Like I told your son when he thought he was dying, there's life in you."

Jean-Louis stood next to her. She noticed his eyes suddenly glisten with the news about his father.

"Let's draw your blood and that will be it."

"Thank you for coming, Françoise," his father murmured.

She heard the same kind of sincere tone in his voice that described his son's. "I'm honored, Louis. You're a man who did all the work after your wife passed away. Few men qualify as a superhero. You're one of them." Add another name to her list of exceptional men.

The older man cleared his throat several times.

Françoise took the gloves out of the packet

and put them on. "Let me push up your sleeve and we'll get this over." Another few minutes and she'd obtained the precious blood.

When she'd finished, she looked around and saw that Jean-Louis's male siblings had come in the room and were staring at her. The three gorgeous brothers together was a heady sight she could scarcely believe. "Am I dreaming, or what?"

They chuckled and nudged Jean-Louis.

Their father pointed to them. "Nic? Raoul? Françoise is here to draw your blood too. I want no argument. Find a place to sit so she can do her job."

Like obedient little boys who knew better than to argue with their father, they did his bidding and made it easy for her. Before long she had three samples of blood and put them in the case.

Smiling at them, she stood up. "Back at the hospital in Nice, when I told Jean-Louis about the procedure, he was afraid I might turn him."

"He's always had a thing about vampires," one of them quipped.

She grinned. "I found that out," she said, thinking of her dream.

At that comment they all burst into laughter. "Thank you so much, gentlemen. I'll take these vials to the hospital now and analyze them. We'll have answers soon. As I told your brother, even if there are abnormalities, you can be assured it's still human blood."

More laughter ensued.

"Stay in bed until tomorrow, Louis. Don't be tempted to get out like your restless son wanted to do at the hospital."

Their father reached out to grasp her hand. "Bless you."

"I'll make sure he stays put," Luca answered with a smile.

Jean-Louis picked up her kit and walked her out, leaving the rest of the family behind them. "You have to be hungry. There's a good restaurant in town."

She shook her head. "Thank you, but I couldn't sit down to a meal right now. Could we pick up something at a deli maybe?"

"I know the exact one. They make tasty meat pies."

"That sounds perfect. We can eat on the way to the hospital."

Twice now they'd eaten in the car. Was that

her way of letting him know she was all business so he wouldn't think she wanted something more from him?

After they left the château and got in the car, she removed her mask and gloves. He put the kit in the back seat. "How long will it take to analyze the samples?"

"Since I know what I'm looking for, we'll have some if not all the answers tonight."

He started the engine and they took off in the semidarkness. "Did you mean what you said about my father's condition?"

"He had good color and seems to be in better shape than I would have imagined. Maybe having been reunited with you, his body is responding to moments of spiritual rejuvenation."

"You think that's possible?"

"I do because I've seen what pure happiness can do for some patients."

After stopping for meat pies and coffee, they ate during the short trip to the hospital.

"Mmm. That filled the bill, Jean-Louis. Thank you. Now I can get right to work."

More than ever, he got the idea she'd only come to La Racineuse as a medical doctor. He ought to be relieved, but instead it disturbed him so much he could hardly think.

They hurried inside to the lab. "I'm staying in here with you."

"Of course. Go ahead and sit at that desk over there. No one else is here right now. This won't take me long."

Watching Françoise at home in her world came as a revelation to Jean-Louis. This woman's knowledge and years of study humbled him. Despite his personal frustration, her delightful bedside manner with his father and brothers had elated him.

During the exam, he'd shared a glance with Corinne, who'd noticed their father's improved condition. Even a temporary reprieve was a reason to rejoice.

While Françoise worked now, he took some pictures of her with his phone camera. When he couldn't be with her, he'd be able to look at them and remember this night of nights. A month ago, he'd thought he was dying. Back then a miracle like this night wouldn't have been a possibility in his mind.

Sooner than he'd imagined, she turned her face to him, wearing a mask and gloves. "I have the best news. None of your family has

PV or anything else. *You* are the only one. Chances are you won't pass it on to any boys you might have one day."

He shot out of the chair. Joy filled him that his brothers and father didn't have his problem. "So, I'm the freak."

"Yup."

"You're one in a million too, Françoise."

She averted her eyes. The woman had trouble accepting praise. "Give me five minutes to clean up everything. Then we'll go back to the château and make the big announcement."

They left the hospital without her wearing a mask or gloves, and arrived home in record time. Jean-Louis found his brothers in the bedroom talking with their father. Their heads turned to see him and Françoise walk in. They couldn't take their eyes off her. No man could.

"*I'm* the only one with PV." His voice resonated in the room. "You're all good to go."

Relief broke out on their faces. His father wept.

Françoise smiled. "Congratulations, gentlemen, and thank you for your cooperation. This has been a wonderful visit for me. It's truly a privilege to meet all of you. As I told

Jean-Louis, your miraculous birth only happens one in a million times. It's textbook stuff for the medical journals."

"You're kidding—" Nic sounded shocked.

"Ask your little brother."

"Wait till I tell Anelise."

She smiled. "While you celebrate, I'll go up to bed since we'll be flying back to Paris in the morning. Unfortunately, I have patients who are waiting to undergo tests you don't want to know about. *Bonne nuit.*"

Like she did in the hospital in Nice, she ran away before Jean-Louis could stop her. Something was going on with her. Obviously, she didn't want him getting any ideas about her being interested in him other than as a friend. He refused to believe it.

"Is that true?" his father asked. "I thought it was one in ten thousand."

"What?" For a moment Jean-Louis's mind was somewhere else.

"The one-in-a-million chance?"

"Oh. *Oui.* Without the help of fertility drugs, the odds escalate. Whenever you've done anything, Papa, it has always been more spectacular."

His father shook his head, then stared at him

out of watery eyes. "I'm sorry I didn't know about your suffering."

"Enough of that. I didn't know I was ill. Those symptoms came in bits and pieces. Françoise says if I take care of myself, I'll live to a goodly age like all of you."

"Thank heaven, son."

"Thank heaven you're feeling a little better this evening, *mon père*." He leaned down to kiss his forehead.

"Amen," his brothers chimed in.

Raoul looked at him, eyeing him earnestly. "Little brother? What's the story on Dr. Valmy?"

Jean-Louis knew what Raoul was asking. He'd like the answer himself, but he didn't have one yet. In the silence, Nic and their father were also waiting. "She was my doctor, but no longer."

"And?" Raoul prodded.

Deep down he knew Françoise was in search of answers and living in a world of pain. For the time being, the reason for it would have to stay privileged information he had no right to divulge. The two of them had developed a strong connection, but Jean-

Louis wasn't on her mind at the moment. He couldn't live with that much longer.

"And nothing. I have to get her back in the morning. That's all. *Bonne nuit, tout le monde.*"

"Wait, Jean-Louis," his father called to him in a surprisingly strong voice.

He wheeled around. "What is it, Papa?"

Louis sat forward. "You can't leave yet. I have things to say to you. First of all, I'm giving you the garage. Other families on the estate have wanted it, but it has always had your stamp on it. Do whatever you want with it since it's empty."

Jean-Louis knew that these days the estate vehicles and machinery were repaired in town. "That's very generous, Papa, but—"

"I'm not finished, *mon fils.*" Jean-Louis hadn't seen this coming. "Now that you're home again and needed here in every way, don't forget about the land I gave you years ago. It's still waiting for you."

Nic grasped Jean-Louis's shoulder. "Anelise and I would love it if you built your own place near Raoul's and we were all neighbors together. You could teach the Causcelle kids how to fix cars."

He nodded. "It's an exciting idea, whether they be boys or girls. The women in the military could do it all."

"Just like the women on this estate who've always been able to do everything," Raoul murmured. A lot of personal pain went into his remark.

Jean-Louis cleared his throat with difficulty. "I love the idea of it too. And marriage or no marriage, I plan to do any job you want me to do on the estate from now on. But as for building a home, you've got to have a wife in order to plan one." For the time being that wasn't the case for Jean-Louis, and maybe not for Raoul. Only time would tell about their futures.

"You don't have to have a woman to make plans," his father asserted.

"You're right, Papa, and your generosity astounds me. But before I can think about anything else, I've been working on a project. In fact, I wanted to talk to you about it, but this isn't the right time."

"Of course it is!" his father came back. "Come sit by me and tell me what's on your mind."

He did his bidding. "It's an idea I thought

about nonstop while I was in the military. But it really hit me hard when my transport plane flew into Nice and dropped me off. After ten years I was back on French soil. I tried to put myself in the place of any returning vet who had nothing to return to."

"We should have been there for you," Nic muttered.

"My selfishness made that impossible, didn't it?"

"Let's not go there." This from Raoul. "Tell us your idea."

"Because I'd been discharged, I at least had a hospital to go to where they took care of me for two weeks. But what of the thousands of the walking wounded getting off transports everywhere? How would the poor devils live now without family or promised work? Where would they turn? Who would hire them?"

Raoul shook his head. "I haven't been where you've been, but I hear you."

"The only money I've used for ten years has been my army pay. But after you and Nic found me and we were all reunited, I—"

"You want to do something with your family money," Nic broke in on him. "You think we don't get it? That's what drove me to want to build free hospitals with research centers."

"Of course."

"How can I help?" his father asked.

He sucked in his breath. "It's very ambitious."

Raoul smiled. "Only successful plans are."

"I've stayed in touch with half a dozen vets. They were in my company for three years before going home and we became friends. They're destitute with no college education or family help. They've been wounded mentally and physically in war. After one job, then another, they're let go. It crushes me to compare my circumstances to theirs."

"Tell us your idea, *mon fils*."

"All right. Since none of our family stays at the *palais* anymore, I'd like permission to use it for a hotel/halfway house for these vets. Naturally I'd set two suites aside for family use when necessary. But there would be ten suites standing empty."

"Just waiting for needy vets," Raoul filled in.

"Yes. Bed and food for free."

Nic stared hard at him. "It's inspirational."

Françoise had said the same thing.

"I'd fund their schooling in Paris and help them get scholarships. When they're certified to work, I'd place them in any city in France where they'd like to be employed. They'd start to earn a decent wage so they can live a good life and raise families. This first group would be the beginning of more. But I know that's too presumptuous and I have no right to ask."

Their father sat there with his head bowed for a long moment. Then he lifted it and his eyes pierced Jean-Louis's.

"Serving in the military for ten years did more to teach you about life than all the prestigious business degrees could ever have done. I've never been more proud of anyone in my life. You've found your *raison d'être*. I want you to take over the *palais* and anything else you need with my blessing. If your mother were here…" His voice trembled.

Jean-Louis reached for his father and hugged him for a long time. "There's no one like you, Papa." When he let him go, his father's eyes were closed and he looked like he had finally fallen asleep.

The three of them said good-night to Luca and left the room. Overjoyed that his brothers were totally on board with his ideas, Jean-Louis went to the kitchen with them to enjoy a cup of coffee.

Near midnight they were all ready for bed. Jean-Louis hugged them and hurried upstairs past Françoise's suite. Much as he longed to share his news with her, it would have to wait until morning during their flight back to Paris.

He also had an idea he wanted to run by her before he took her back to her apartment. She'd probably fight him on it, but it was worth a try.

CHAPTER SIX

AFTER BREAKFAST ON board the Causcelle jet with Jean-Louis, Françoise realized that this interlude of being treated like a princess was fast coming to an end. She'd loved being in his world for a little while and regretted that it was over.

As they talked during the flight, his black eyes came alive. He told her that his dreams for helping vets were going to come true now that he'd had the important talk with his father and family. He also explained that he'd be living on the family estate and working there from now on. It meant he'd only be in Paris once in a while to check on his project.

Since she'd been given a week's freedom to plan out her life, she'd made up her mind to drive to Bourges and check out the hospital there. If she were hired, that would mean no more chance meetings with Jean-Louis.

His latest news shouldn't have bothered her, but it did in ways she was afraid to acknowledge. Much as she longed to be with him, a relationship with him was out of the question right now.

"Françoise?"

She glanced at him.

"You've been wonderful to my family, but I know there's a pain inside of you that won't be going away soon. I've given it a lot of thought and an idea came to my mind during the night. Do you live by a certain faith, or go to a certain church?"

His question astonished her coming out of the blue as it did. "Yes. Our family is Catholic."

"So's mine, although I stopped going years ago." She could understand that since she hadn't gone for a long time either. "Did your parents have you baptized at a church here in Paris?"

"Yes. My great-aunt is my godmother and witnessed it. That's why we've been so close."

"What if we stop by there on the way to your apartment and talk to the priest? Trying to get information online won't tell you anything. But if you see him in person, maybe he can show you the written document, or answer some of your questions. It's possible that he or someone else in the clergy who knew your parents could shed some light on the adoption for you."

She sucked in her breath. "You're brilliant to have thought of that, Jean-Louis. I don't know why it hadn't occurred to me to go there for answers right away."

"I'm sure you would have thought of it at some point. But remember, you just took your boards. And you've had too much on your mind with your move back here and helping my family."

"Thank you for being in my corner. The truth is, I haven't been to church for ages. No wonder it wasn't my first thought."

"That's one thing we have in common," he murmured.

"Actually, we have three," she claimed. "Neither of us knew our birth mother. And neither of us told each other the whole truth about ourselves right off."

He shook his head. "My lie was premeditated ten years ago."

"But I've been claiming to be a Valmy *all* my life."

"Unpremeditated doesn't count, Françoise. Maybe you'll find an answer you can live with before the day is out." The Fasten Seat Belts sign flashed on. "We're about ready to land. When we get in the limo, shall I tell our driver to take us to your apartment or the church?"

She buckled up. "You didn't need to ask that question since you already know the answer. It's on the Rue des Moines." Every time she was ready to say goodbye to him— wishing it wouldn't be their last—something else came up that pulled her in to him again.

Before long they'd been picked up and Jean-Louis told the driver where to take them. When they'd pulled up in the church parking area, he turned to her. "Since this is a totally private matter, would you like to go in alone? If so, I'll stay in the limo."

Françoise appreciated his consideration. In fact, there wasn't anything about him or his behavior she didn't like. Except that *like* wasn't the right word. She didn't dare say the word that fit her true feelings.

"Please come in with me. It was your idea and I can't thank you enough."

He got out to help her and they walked to

the side door that let them into the church office. A middle-aged woman seated at a rectangular table greeted them and asked them to be seated. She wore a tag that said Annette Larue. *"Bon après-midi.* How can I help you?"

Françoise sat forward. "Twenty-eight years ago, on February 10, I was born and eventually baptized in this church. Do you keep the original document here? I'd like to see it if I could."

"I'll consult the parish register. Please fill out this form and I'll take care of it." She handed Françoise a clipboard with a pen and the attached paper.

It didn't take Françoise long to write down the information. She handed it back to the other woman.

"I'll go into the archive room and be right back."

"Merci, madame."

After the woman left, Françoise looked at Jean-Louis. "This seems too easy."

Those black eyes gazed steadily into hers. "That's because your baptism didn't need to be hidden."

"I know. I'm being ridiculous."

"Not at all. Once you've verified everything, we'll look at the name of the priest officiating. Then you can ask to talk to him. Maybe he'll remember something that will help you."

"That is if he's still serving at this church." Then a groan escaped. She lowered her eyes. "Forgive me, Jean-Louis. I'm behaving like a fractious child."

He reached over and gave her hand a little squeeze. "You have every reason to be anxious." His support comforted her. Without his help, she wouldn't even have thought to come to the church.

"Here we are." The woman walked back to the table carrying the cumbersome register. "I found the correct volume." She put it on the table in front of them and opened it to the right place. "Please be careful. These pages are fragile."

"Of course." Françoise examined everything. "Oh, Jean-Louis—look at that handwriting."

He sat closer to inspect it. "A lost art these days."

"I can't believe it. This is the original document." She couldn't prevent the tremor in her voice. "'Parents: Patrick and Dionne Valmy. Infant daughter: Marie Françoise Valmy. Godmother: Nadine Bonnet. Priest officiating: Father Alexis Marquette.'"

"Is the name Marie significant?"

She nodded to him. "My grandmother's first name."

He took another breath. "Do you remember hearing the name of that priest?" Jean-Louis whispered.

"No. It means nothing to me."

She looked up at the other woman. "Can I please make an appointment to speak with Father Alexis Marquette?"

"I'm sorry, but he died two years ago."

No... Her heart sank. She fought not to break down. "He was the one who baptized me." Devastated because another door had just shut in her face, she closed the register.

"Father Benoit could talk to you."

"No. He wouldn't be able to answer my questions... But thank you."

In the next breath Jean-Louis got to his feet. "Thank you for helping us, *madame*. We won't take up any more of your time."

Françoise murmured her thanks before he took hold of her arm and walked her outside to the limo. Without his help, she doubted she could have walked out on her own.

He gave the driver the address to her apartment and they drove away. Earlier on the jet when he'd talked about them visiting the church, she'd been filled with hope. Now that it was dashed, she felt numb inside. *And ashamed.*

It was too embarrassing for her to imagine what Jean-Louis must think of her. She might be a grown woman and a doctor, but she couldn't handle what life had handed her with even a modicum of grace.

"This doesn't have to be the end of your search, Françoise. At the time you were born, did your father have a confidant or best friend? What about your mother? Think back."

"They must have had a close friend or two, but none I remember from that long ago."

"Have you kept some of their memorabilia?"

"Maman saved things in a box. It's in storage at the moving company I used."

"Here in Paris?"

"Yes."

"Why don't you pick it up and go through everything? Who knows what you might find?"

She lifted her head. "You mean now?"

"I don't see why not. I can't see you getting much sleep later tonight, and closing time won't be for another hour. When we reach the apartment, you can leave for the moving company in your car. Before you go to bed, you may have found a photo of a friend or someone who can shed light on what happened."

"Oh, if I thought that were true…" This man was a marvel. "Would you come with me?" Françoise had said it so automatically, she shocked herself.

Jean-Louis almost jumped out of his skin with excitement. The concern in those gorgeous green eyes slayed him. "What do you think?"

"You really don't mind?"

Mind? For the first time since he'd known her, Françoise had asked him to do something *with* her. It had nothing to do with her being a doctor, or her trying to help him. "I'll ask the driver to take us there right now. What's the name of the company?"

"Gilbert Demenagement. It's not too far from the hospital where I work."

He spoke through the intercom to give the driver directions. In a few minutes they arrived at the moving company. Jean-Louis asked the driver to wait and they went inside. When the box had been brought out, he carried it to the limo and they headed for her apartment.

Once there, she brought in her overnight bag while Jean-Louis took care of the box. He told the driver to leave and followed her to the second floor, where she lived.

She put down her bag. "As you can see, this furnished apartment isn't the *palais*, but it's close to my work and convenient until I can find my own place. Several of the hospital staff live here too."

Jean-Louis had been so preoccupied with thoughts of her wanting his help, he scarcely noticed the surroundings. "After the army, this apartment *is* a palace."

She turned to him. "How do I thank you? I hardly know where to begin after what you've done for me. I know you're anxious to get back to your project and the limo is still waiting for you."

"No, it isn't. I told him to leave. It's too late for me to work on anything tonight. I saw your face at the church when you heard the priest had died. I felt your pain and I'd like to help you learn the truth about the adoption. It's the least I can do after you brought me back to life."

Her velvety green eyes filled with tears. "I'm so glad you want to stay. The thought of going through that box alone—" But she couldn't finish.

"I know. When the taxi drove me along the Promenade des Anglais after I got off the transport plane, the sight of the Causcelle Prom Hotel almost destroyed me. The memories of my former life flew at me, and the only thing that saved me at that moment was knowing I'd come home to die."

"Oh, Jean-Louis. You understand better than anyone else in the world could."

Without conscious thought, only need, he drew her into his arms and she sobbed quietly against his chest. He rocked her as she clung to him. Holding her felt so right, he never wanted to let her go. The fragrance of her hair and skin, the feel of her against his body—nothing compared to the feelings and sensations she aroused in him. But a sudden loud knocking on the door broke his trance.

Françoise pulled away from him. "Jacques?" she called out. He assumed it was the concierge. "Is there a fire or a burst pipe?"

"No," a wintry male voice answered. "It's Eric."

Jean-Louis's body tensed.

"But how did you get in the building?"

"I have my ways. Open the door. We have to talk."

She walked over to it. "Lower your voice. We've said everything there is to say."

"No, we haven't!" he countered. "You told me there wasn't anyone else, but you've been lying to me. I saw a man come in here with you a few minutes ago and he hasn't left. I'd like an explanation."

"We've said our goodbyes, Eric, and I have a guest with me."

"Are you going to make me wait out here?"

Jean-Louis walked over to her. "Eric sounds more than determined," he whispered. "If you want me to deal with this, I will." The other man was crazy in love with Françoise. That much was obvious.

He heard her sharp intake of breath. "No, I'll let him in, but stay with me."

That was music to his ears. "I'll sit on the

couch while you talk." He sank down in the middle and waited for her to open the door.

Eric walked in and almost stumbled over her overnight bag. "Where have you been, Françoise? I've been calling this apartment and your phone for two days!"

"I had to go out of town overnight on a case and just got back. Why are you here?"

"You know why." His glacial gaze flew to Jean-Louis, then back at her. "What's going on?"

"I've been attending this man's father, who's ill."

"That's a good story. Where's the patient now?"

She folded her arms. "Eric—what do you want?"

"I want to talk to you. *Alone*. I have the right."

"We've said our goodbyes."

"But I *haven't*! So, this man's going to spend another night with you? How many have there been during the time I was working in Rabat?"

Jean-Louis had heard enough and got to his feet. "I don't think we've ever met." He walked over to Eric, not a bad-looking man if he weren't torn up with jealousy. "I know you're a Moreau. I'm Jean-Louis Causcelle."

His head flew back. He studied him. "That face is familiar. You *are* one of the Causcelle triplets."

"That's right. I was discharged from the army a month ago with an illness that Dr. Valmy found and diagnosed in Nice. She flew to my home in La Racineuse to attend my father, who's dying of heart failure. He wanted to know if he has my blood disorder. It turns out he doesn't. We just flew back to Paris. I offered to help her with that box over there before leaving."

"Your disappearance turned this country upside down." Clearly he hadn't heard a word of Jean-Louis's explanation.

Eric switched his gaze to Françoise and stared at her through narrowed lids. "Well, well, well. I *was* right. You did find someone else with a lot more money than I could ever make, even when elected."

Elected? That's right. Antoine had told Jean-Francois the man would be running for president of the country.

"Who else but a Causcelle with his billions? *Bonne chance, cherie.*" Eric flew out the door.

Jean-Louis stepped forward and closed it. In his gut he knew the man was out of her life permanently, *grâce à Dieu.*

"Jean-Louis?" She sounded fragmented.

He turned to her. "Nothing needs to be said. I'm immune. The poor devil is in love and hurting, just like Antoine." There wasn't a woman on the planet like Françoise. No one knew it better than Jean-Louis. "You need to dig into that box and forget everything else."

After a long pause, "You're right. If you'd like to freshen up in the bathroom down the hall, I'll fix us some coffee and get started."

"You're reading my mind."

A few minutes later he walked into the living room where she'd put their mugs of coffee on the table in front of the couch. She'd pulled the box over to one end and knelt on the floor.

He took a seat near her and started to drink the coffee while she sorted through various old photos and keepsakes. "I don't see any recognizable people in these old group pictures. No letters. But here are my parents' framed certificates and awards. I don't think I'm going to find a clue in here after all."

Jean-Louis leaned forward to look through them. One caught his eye. "Didn't you say your parents went to medical school in Paris?"

"Yes."

"How come this internship certificate on your father says Asclepius Hospital in Rouen?"

"What?"

"An appropriate name for a hospital, don't you think? Wasn't Asclepius the son of the god Apollo, known for healing?"

She shook her beautiful head. "How do you know so much about an obscure piece of Greek mythology?"

"One of my high school teachers was big on it. Here. Take another look."

Françoise took it back from him and studied it for a moment. "I can't believe I didn't notice this. According to the date here, Papa must have done a rotation at this hospital after they were married." Her brows furrowed. "But Maman never mentioned anything about them being separated. I guess she went with him. I'm surprised."

"Maybe that's worth investigating," he declared.

She looked up at him. Hope radiated from those divine green orbs. "What would I do without you, Jean-Louis? All these things have been in this box for years. If you hadn't suggested looking at some memorabilia, let alone catching this, I would have missed it completely. Now that you've discovered it, I need to talk to the administrator at that hospital."

He got to his feet. A surge of hope swept through him. She sounded as if she wouldn't mind spending more time with him. When he'd held her in his arms earlier, maybe she'd felt its rightness too. "If you can take one more day off from work, why don't I drive us there tomorrow? We'll give your car a rest."

"Oh, no. You've done too much for me already."

"I have a selfish reason since Rouen is one of the cities where I intend to make some contacts for my project. I'm also as anxious as you to find the answer to your adoption. Now would be the perfect time to do both."

She sprang to her feet. "Why don't I talk to Dr. Soulis first thing in the morning, and then phone you."

In that moment she failed to meet his eyes,

166 FALLING FOR HER SECRET BILLIONAIRE

giving him a frisson of fear. Was she putting him off?

"I have no doubts he'll say yes." Since her boss had been in touch with her for a whole year before she took her boards, he was probably in love with her too. Upset, Jean-Louis pulled out his phone and called for a taxi before walking to the door.

Françoise followed him. "Figuratively speaking, you've become my knight in shining armor. I hope you realize that."

What was she saying now? His desire to crush her in his arms and make love to her was all he wanted to do, but he would have to wait a while longer. "Since you literally saved my life, I'd say we're even. Get a good sleep, Françoise. Perhaps tomorrow will bring the end to your pain."

Françoise watched his incredible physique walk out the door to the elevator and disappear. She hadn't wanted him to leave. When he'd held her in his arms earlier to comfort her, she'd known then she never wanted him to let her go.

She was no different from Celestine or Suzanne, or all the women written about in the newspapers who clamored to be with one of the gorgeous Causcelle triplets. Even Eric, who could be tough as nails in a political fight, backed off the second he recognized him. No man could compete with Robert Martin, who'd become her modern-day Adonis.

After Jean-Louis had talked to her about the name of the hospital in Rouen, another Greek myth had flashed through her mind.

In Zeus's household, the goddess Aphrodite had protected the beautiful Adonis and had appointed Persephone to raise him. But Persephone fell in love with Adonis and refused to give him back to Aphrodite. Zeus stepped in. He ordered Adonis to spend a third of a year with each of the two goddesses, and a third with whichever one he wanted. In the end Adonis chose to spend two-thirds of each year with Aphrodite and had two children with her.

Would that Françoise could be Jean-Louis's Aphrodite and give him children one day. But right there her fantasy had to stop! She was living in a nightmare, not a myth. Once she'd found a place to work and live near her great-aunt, she'd leave Paris and never see Jean-Louis again. That's why she'd deliberately lied to him about needing permission to get off work. She needed to protect them both.

Françoise Valmy, or whatever your real name might have been, you can't be with any man until you have answers as to why your father hid that specially sealed adoption paper in his bag. Your whole life is in question. Don't inflict possible pain on Jean-Louis. The last thing he needs is to be associated with a woman whose father's illegal actions had to be hidden from the world. Once exposed, the result could be disastrous if it put a stain on the Valmy name.

Dr. Soulis had given her a week off to deal with her life. There was no time like the present to get going. But when she reached for her laptop to look at a map and plan her trip to Bourges, she realized she'd left it at the lab. The only thing to do was run by the hospital in the morning before leaving Paris.

Tonight, she would pack enough clothes for a week that might also include a trip to Rouen to do some digging. In her heart, however, she feared it would be a wasted journey with no results.

Before long she went to bed only to spend the most restless night of her life reliving her day. Françoise had been so off-balance around Jean-Louis, she'd clung to him. The memory still brought heat to her face. In fact, she'd said and done things that let him think she craved his company. Heaven knew she did, but that behavior couldn't be allowed to go on. No more Jean-Louis ever.

Awakening early the next morning, she dressed quickly and carried her suitcase out to the car. En route to the hospital for her laptop, she stopped at a café for breakfast. While she ate, she texted Jean-Louis, explaining that she couldn't get away because they were swamped at work. She couldn't ask Dr. Soulis for another favor. After thanking Jean-Louis for everything he'd done, she wished him well on his project.

As soon as she pressed the send button, she felt like she'd just cut the invisible tether that had joined them from the beginning. Now she was the one dangling out in the vast void of space. Since he'd come into her life, she'd welcomed every day because he inhabited her universe. With him gone from her life, Françoise knew she'd never be truly happy again and better get used to it.

Once at the hospital, she dashed inside and

found her laptop in the drawer of her desk. So far there'd been no activity on her phone to suggest that Jean-Louis had texted her back. Good. He'd gotten the message and was leaving well enough alone. With her heart feeling like a lodestone, she started for the door just as Celestine came running into the lab.

"Oh, good—it's *you*, Dr. Valmy! Do you remember about that gorgeous vet who came without an appointment?"

More déjà vu.

Just the thought of Jean-Louis sent shivers of longing through her. "Yes?"

"He has come again without an appointment and is asking for *you*."

Her body quickened. This meant he'd seen her text and wasn't happy about it. "I'm afraid I'm far too busy, but I passed Dr. Loudat's office on my way down the hall. Ask him. He'll do the procedure."

"All right." She looked dejected. "I'd hoped he'd come in early to see me, but no such luck. Whoever he's crazy about has to be the luckiest woman on earth."

Celestine knew what she was talking about. "Never fear. Someone wonderful will come along for you one day."

"But he'll never be this guy."

You're right.

"Have a good one, Dr. Valmy."

"You too."

Celestine walked away. The second she disappeared, Françoise ran out thc cxit door at the other end of the lab and raced down five flights of stairs. Halfway to her car she saw Jean-Louis stride toward her looking incredible in chinos and a blazer. Those eyes of his reminded her of black fires. "I'm glad I caught you before you left on your busy day."

She swallowed hard. "Why didn't you answer my text? I could have saved you this trip."

"Your text let me know you were running away again. It's your pattern."

His comment brought her up short and guilt took over. She looked around. "Could we talk in my car so people can't hear us?"

"I insist on it."

Françoise struggled for breath. His mood left no room for argument. This was a new side to him. She opened the door and climbed in. He walked over to the passenger door, which she unlocked with the remote. Jean-Louis got in without problem since he'd adjusted the seat the other day to accommodate his long, powerful legs. Then he turned to her.

"I see your suitcase in the back seat and want the truth from you. Every time I think we're enjoying each other's company a little more, you manage to slip away. I know in my gut there's an attraction between us, but something is stopping you from getting any closer to me. Why?"

Her stomach muscles tightened, preventing her from answering him.

"When I believed I was dying, Françoise, you convinced me I wasn't. I'd like you to convince me now of the real reason you canceled our plans for today. I can take your truth, but I need to hear it. You're a doctor and should understand that better than anyone."

She gripped the edge of her seat, unable to look at him. "If an adoption document can be specially sealed, it can also be specially unsealed under certain circumstances. I live in fear of its secret being exposed one day, Jean-Louis, and it will! Trust me on this. Whatever my parents wanted concealed forever, let's agree that there's no such thing as forever. When I learn the painful truth, I don't want it to affect anyone else."

He slid his arm across the back of her seat and gently massaged her neck. She wished he hadn't done that. His touch sent bursts of desire through her body. "So that means you're not going to let me into your life any further while you wait for that terrifying day?"

"I can't!" she cried. "Don't you see? You've endured a lifetime of notoriety and illness up to now. I won't involve you or any man in my painful personal battle, no matter what it may be."

"Even if the truth should come out forty years from now?"

"That's right. A single life hurts no one else."

She felt his body constrict before he removed his arm, denying her the closeness that thrilled her to the very core. "Do you honestly think your parents would want that life for you?"

"I'm not sure. It's possible my adoptive father left the adoption paper in his bag on purpose. Maybe he hoped I'd find it one day and eventually learn its ugly secret. I've thought about it a lot."

"That doesn't make sense. Your parents loved you."

"Hear me out, Jean-Louis. Perhaps my birth mother and father have been trying to find me all these years, but they can't put their hands on the sealed document to learn who adopted me. What if my adoptive parents feared something bad could happen if they did find me? So, they decided to leave the document for me to discover, knowing I'd investigate."

"Why would they do that?"

"Maybe it was their way of warning me of something terrible before my birth parents caught up to me."

He let out a sound of exasperation. "Since all this has been building inside of you, why aren't you eager to go to Rouen with me right now?"

"I plan to, but I have to do it alone on my own time."

"After all you've done for me, is there no way you'll allow me to help you now?"

The hurt and frustration in his voice cut her to the very soul, but she had no choice. Françoise had to push him away for his own sake and hers. "Kind as you are because it's in your nature, I—I don't want your help," she stammered. "We should never have met." She closed her eyes tightly. "I'd hoped the text I sent to you this morning had said it all."

In the next instant she heard his door open and her heart lurched. "You accomplished your objective, Françoise. The problem is, I didn't want to accept it because there's a bond between us, and I know you feel it too. That's why you run and keep running."

Without saying another word, he got out of the car and shut the door. She sat there in a cocoon of pain while he walked to the Mercedes.

CHAPTER SEVEN

Jean-Louis drove straight to the *palais*, experiencing an agony that was totally foreign to him. Since adulthood he'd avoided all serious relationships with women until Françoise had come into his life. This morning he'd reached out, and she'd cut through him with the precision of a surgical knife.

Kind as you are, because it's in your nature, I—I don't want your help. We should never have met.

Rejection for something normal, like she didn't have romantic feelings for him, was one thing. But she *did* want him the way he wanted her. He'd felt it when he'd held her in his arms at her apartment. Though sobbing, she'd clung to him like they were two halves of a whole. Only the shocking news that she'd been adopted had flung her into such a dark place, the true Françoise had been buried alive and was unreachable.

He knew in every atom of his body she'd never let him get close to her again until she had answers. He could imagine her living a lifetime alone waiting for them. But it wouldn't take that long if he had anything to say about it. There was only one thing to do.

After arriving at the *palais*, he raced inside his suite and looked on his phone list for the number of Claude Giraud, the retired secret service agent who'd tracked him down. If that man couldn't produce the needed miracle, then Jean-Louis would have to admit defeat and stay unattached because there could be no other woman for him. The one thing he'd been desperate to avoid for years had finally happened. Though he hadn't even kissed Françoise yet, he sensed they were soul mates.

Claude was his only hope, but to his frustration he had to leave his number. It wasn't until early Wednesday morning the other man called him back. Jean-Louis had paced the bedroom floor most of the night. When he heard the ring, he flung himself across the bed to reach his cell on the bedside table. "Claude?"

"*Eh, bien*, Jean-Louis. How is the lost Causcelle who has returned to the fold?"

Jean-Louis liked Claude. "All is well, except for my heart."

"I'm sorry to hear that," he came back in a sincere tone. "Don't tell me you have your father's condition."

His hand tightened on the phone. "*Non.* I'm afraid it's of a different kind, and I need your help. Name any price."

"I'll be very happy to assist. You know that."

"It won't be easy."

"Tell me your problem."

For the next ten minutes he unloaded on Claude all the information he could think of. "I believe the visit to Rouen might be a good place for you to start. Her father did an internship there around the time of the adoption."

"This is good. You've given me a lot to go on."

"Claude—I'm depending on you. She's my life's blood." His throat thickened. "Without her, I don't know if I'll be—"

"Don't say it, Jean-Louis," he cut him off.

"Don't even think it. Give me a month and I'll get back to you."

He groaned. "A month?"

"Probably no longer. This time I won't be hunting for a soldier who wants to remain lost. In the meantime, stay busy, *mon ami. A toute à l'heure.*"

Jean-Louis hung up and forced himself off the bed. Thirty days sounded like an eternity. The only thing to do was get busy right now and fill the *palais* with vets. He would use this time to get them started on their training in any *metier* they wanted. Until Claude got back to him, he needed to put thoughts of Françoise out of his mind. *As if that were possible.*

Françoise spent the next few days in Bouzy at Nadine's bedside, sleeping nights at a nearby hotel. During that time the doctor got her bronchitis under control. However, he told Françoise her great-aunt's emphysema wasn't getting better. He estimated she could live maybe three, four more months, no longer. His news changed everything for her.

Two days later she felt she could leave for part of the day. Getting in her car, she drove the hour-and-quarter distance to Bourges for an arranged interview with the hospital director.

She enjoyed meeting the congenial administrator, who thankfully didn't link her with her father. He took her on a tour of the lab and facilities. Françoise imagined she could be happy enough working there if she had to. Before she left, he offered her the epidemiology position. She said she'd have to think about it and get back to him.

The return trip to Bouzy took longer. By the time she reached the hotel, she realized she didn't want to have to drive close to three hours a day to come and go. She needed to stay in Bouzy with her aunt and find a furnished apartment online.

Once she drove to the address of one to take a look, she ended up paying first and last months' rent on a short-term lease. In the morning she called the hospital administrator in Bourges to tell him she decided she couldn't take the position, but she thanked him profusely for his time.

With that accomplished, she left for Paris to resign her position. She had enough savings to live for six months, if necessary, without working.

First, she moved her few things out of her apartment and cleaned it. Later she canceled her phone number and got a new one. At the end of that day, she met with Christophe and told him the sad news about her great-aunt. He commiserated with her situation and accepted her resignation. She could always apply again one day when circumstances had changed.

Françoise asked him to tell no one why she'd left or what her plans were. She wanted complete privacy. Not that Jean-Louis would ever venture near after what she'd said to him. Christophe assured her of his silence. After a tearful goodbye, she left the City of Lights for Bouzy.

The old season of life had passed away. A new one had begun. She and Nadine would face it together.

Don't be tempted to look back, Françoise.

What a joke. During the drive, she relived every moment with Jean-Louis. Tears trickled down her face to think she'd never know that kind of joy again.

"Hey—Jean-Louis. We're almost filled up."

He flicked his gaze to Guy. They'd been talking at the front desk. Guy had agreed to be in charge of the new vet hostel, and over the last week the man had become his right arm.

"You're right. I'm waiting for Remy, the last one who'll be coming in the van from the airport within the hour. You'll like him. He served under me for a time."

"I like all of them. It's a grand thing you're doing, Jean-Louis. My wife cried over your generosity when I first told her about your plan for the *palais*."

"Thanks, Guy. We'll see if this experiment works out. I couldn't do it without you."

"It's going perfectly, and you're paying me too much."

He shook his head. "Guy? There isn't enough money to compensate you for all you're doing. When I'm back in La Racineuse, I'll be able to do my work on the estate knowing you and the staff have this place running better than the finest Swiss watch."

"It's a pleasure."

"The guys think the world of you too." He patted Guy's shoulder. "Tell you what. I'm going upstairs to make some phone calls. Let me know when he arrives."

"Will do."

He walked down the hall to the elevator

that took him to his suite. He no longer felt guilt that he was the only one living here. None of the men were in the army now, but they had a camaraderie no one else could understand. Guy was getting a taste of it.

He grabbed a cola from the fridge and sat down on the couch to deal with the phone calls that had come in while he'd been setting up a new computer in Remy's room.

With each call, he'd prayed to see Françoise's name to no avail. This evening there were three calls from La Racineuse he needed to return. Halfway through his conversation with Raoul, another call came in. *Claude Giraud!*

Jean-Louis sprang to his feet, coming close to cardiac arrest. He clicked on.

"Claude? *Grâce à Dieu.*"

"Sorry it has taken me this long to get back to you, Jean-Louis. To make a long story short, you'll have noticed on the news that the president of our country has been on a tour and just got back yesterday."

He blinked. "I don't understand."

"The problem you gave me led me from one obstacle to another. It was very unusual. In fact, I would say impossible. I finally realized I needed the highest authority in the land in order to look inside that particular adoption."

Hadn't Françoise said something about that long ago? Jean-Louis could hardly breathe. He started walking around. "What are you saying?"

"I met with the president today and explained your particular situation. The name Dr. Patrick Valmy, plus the name Louis Causcelle, worked magic on my former boss. He holds both men in the very highest regard. In an unprecedented move, he allowed me to look into the adoption brief long enough to understand why it had been specially sealed."

That meant Claude knew everything! Jean-Louis's gut clenched.

"I've been instructed to tell no one but Françoise Valmy what I learned. I can't tell you. Not even the president knows. He trusts me not to violate what he is allowing, or I could be imprisoned. This isn't about politics. It's beyond top secret."

What?

"No one must ever know what I've done. It will be up to Dr. Valmy if she ever tells you. Do you understand what I'm telling you?"

Imprisonment? He leaned against the wall for support. "I hear you."

"If you'll give me her number, I'll get in touch with her tonight."

"Claude?" he said after doing his bidding. "I don't know what to say, or how to thank you for this. You're saving my life."

"I hope that's true for your sake."

The man's choice of words troubled Jean-Louis, but he couldn't worry about that right now. He was too grateful for what Claude had done. "Whatever you should want or need, name it and it's yours."

"I appreciate that. Just remember, not a word to anyone ever, or my life isn't worth a *sou*, let alone the president's."

He heard the click. This time Claude's wording sent a strange tremor through his body. While he tried to absorb the implication in the man's warning, his phone rang. It was Guy. That meant Remy had arrived.

Jean-Louis left the suite to meet the vet and help him get oriented. Before the end of the night, he knew he'd be hearing from Françoise. Whether the news from Claude brought her happiness or dreaded pain, her wait would be over. Though she'd declined his help earlier, she would feel obligated to call Jean-Louis. Just the thought of hearing her voice again sent a lightning bolt through him, bringing him to life once more.

An hour later he said good-night to Remy and headed for his suite. Unable to settle down, he returned the calls from La Racineuse while he waited for his phone to ring. Five minutes after he and Raoul had finished talking, he saw Claude Giraud's name on the incoming call.

He grabbed his cell. "Claude?"

"I'm glad you answered. Will you give me Dr. Valmy's phone number again? I must have written it down wrong."

Jean-Louis groaned inwardly. The former agent hadn't even talked to her yet? "Here it is." He repeated it slowly. Claude thanked him and they hung up. Two minutes later he rang him again and he picked up. "Claude?"

"Sorry, Jean-Louis, but it's no longer her number. I checked with the phone company. As soon as you get the new one from her, let me know and I'll call her immediately."

She was still running from him. "Thank you, Claude. You'll be hearing from me soon."

The only thing to do was drive over to her

apartment. Even if it was after ten, he would have to disturb the landlord because this constituted an emergency. Five minutes later he reached the complex, but saw no sign of her car. A visit with the man named Jacques and he learned she'd moved out two weeks ago with no forwarding address.

His frustration off the charts, Jean-Louis returned to the *palais*. After a shower, he went to bed and spent a sleepless night. At six he got up and dressed before taking off for her place of work. Though he didn't see her car in the hospital parking, it didn't matter since she probably wouldn't arrive until eight. He went inside and waited for her in the fifth-floor lounge. Two cups of coffee later, he approached an older nurse at the desk who'd just arrived. He'd seen her before.

"How soon do you expect Dr. Valmy?"

"I'm sorry, *monsieur*. Dr. Valmy doesn't work here anymore."

The news ripped his insides apart. "Since when?"

"I believe she left two weeks ago."

This couldn't be happening. "Do you know where she's working now?"

"I don't. I believe you're the vet who came

in to get your blood drawn a while back. What can I do to help you this morning?"

He needed to get a grip. "Is Dr. Soulis here? I must talk to him. It's an emergency."

"I'll see if he's available." She made a call and a short conversation ensued before she hung up. "Dr. Soulis will be right out."

"Thank you." He paced in front of the desk until Françoise's sixtyish-looking former boss appeared.

"I understand you wanted to talk to me. The nurse mentioned an emergency."

"It is. Dr. Valmy was my doctor in Nice before she moved here. I have to talk to her."

"Unfortunately, she's no longer available. I'll be happy to recommend another doctor in her field to help you."

Anger kindled inside him. "You don't understand. I need *her*. Where is she working now?"

His hands opened. "I have no idea."

Jean-Louis got the feeling the other man could be speaking the truth. No doubt Françoise had told her boss to say nothing. "Do you at least have a phone number for her? It's vital."

"I have no information on Dr. Valmy since she left our employ." Of course not. "I'm sorry."

So am I.

"Thank you for your time, Dr. Soulis." Jean-Louis wheeled around and left the hospital.

Once in his car, he phoned Claude and told him of Françoise's disappearance. "Can you do me one more favor and find out her new phone number?"

"I wish I could, but I made a vow to the president. No more investigation on this case that could leave tracks, if you know what I mean."

His eyes closed tightly. "Forgive me. I'm desperate."

"I know you won't give up trying to find her. I'll be waiting for your call."

He clicked off, leaving Jean-Louis frantic.

The only tie Françoise valued in her dark place lived at the rest home in Bouzy-la-Forêt. In another two hours he could be there. First, he would go back to the *palais* to throw some things together in a duffel bag. He might have to stay in the village for a few nights.

Thirty minutes later he took off on the A-6 headed south. En route, he talked with Guy and answered several calls from the registrar enrolling Remy in a beginning EMT program. Everything in Paris seemed to be going well by the time he drove into Bouzy and found the Silver Pines rest home.

Searching all around, he couldn't see Françoise's car, but for once he wasn't alarmed. She would never leave her godmother. He'd stop at the L'Auberge for a meal, then drive over to the rest home to wait for her.

Today was Nadine's eighty-sixth birthday. Françoise left the store with another jigsaw puzzle to help with dementia. It would fit on the overbed table. This one featured eight famous French châteaux for her great-aunt to identify. One of them turned out to be the Causcelle family home and gardens in La Racineuse. Françoise melted at the sight of it and she couldn't resist buying it. That visit had changed her life, leaving her with an aching sense of loss that would never go away.

She'd also purchased Nadine's favorite snacks at the grocery store so they could celebrate. Françoise would have loved to bring her red roses, her godmother's favorite flower, but she'd developed a serious allergy to pollen. Françoise had also chosen foods that were good for her while she battled emphysema.

The day wore on as they munched on grapes and nuts. Nadine only nodded over three of the châteaux on the box though she'd visited all of them but one.

Françoise pointed to it. "This château located in Eastern France was deeded to the Causcelle family in 1200. I went there to see a patient with a heart condition."

"Sad," her godmother murmured.

"Yes. Louis Causcelle is a remarkable man."

Suddenly Nadine looked up at Françoise, struggling to say something. The word finally came out. "Triplets?"

Françoise almost fell out of the chair. "Yes. You remembered his name! Three triplet sons."

Just then Thea poked her head inside the door. "You have a visitor on your special day, Nadine. Is it all right?"

"She'd love it, Thea." Françoise glanced at her great-aunt. "I bet it's your friend Fria from down the hall."

"No." Thea shook her head. "It's a man I've never seen before, but he says he knows you."

"What's his name?"

"He wants it to be a surprise."

"Oh. I bet it's my landlady's son, Fabien. She said she would send him over with some *pains au chocolat* for Nadine's birthday. Tell him to come in."

When Jean-Louis walked in the room looking jaw-droppingly gorgeous in a heather-blue suit, she thought she was hallucinating.

Those black eyes blazed as they took in every inch of her, making her feel faint. "It's good to see you, Françoise." His deep voice permeated the room. He walked over to the end of the hospital bed. "I've wanted to meet your great-aunt. Nadine Bonnet, isn't it? The nurse said she's recovering from her bronchitis. I'm glad to hear it. I'm Jean-Louis Causcelle, Nadine. It's a real pleasure to meet you."

Her godmother lifted her hand and pointed at him. "Triplet."

His low chuckle invaded Françoise's body. "Yes. I'm the youngest one. Happy birthday. It looks like I've interrupted you putting a puzzle together."

Françoise's cheeks turned to flame when he leaned over to look at the lid of the puzzle. "May I help? I haven't done a puzzle in years." He reached for a chair and pulled it up to the other side of the bed.

Nothing could have shocked Françoise more when her great-aunt smiled at him and nodded. He knew all about her condition. While he fit puzzle pieces together, he just kept talking as if it were the most natural thing in the world that she didn't answer.

"I've been busy helping returned veterans from war get settled into schools to train them for work. Ten of them now live where I live in the Marais district of Paris. You know when Françoise came out to La Racineuse to take care of my father and draw his blood, I took some photos of her working in the hospital lab there." She gasped in more surprise. "I'd like to give them to you for a birthday present."

In the next instant he produced six small photos showing Françoise checking out the blood samples. Her great-aunt studied them before staring at Françoise. She put a hand to her own face. "Mask."

He laughed. "I don't like it when she wears one either. It hides her beauty."

Most amazing to Françoise was the touching way she put her hand on his to thank him for the gift. Françoise knew she was going to cry. "Excuse me for a moment." She jumped up and hurried out to the hall. After giving way to tears, she wiped her eyes and went back to the room.

Jean-Louis just kept on talking about life at La Racineuse and the rose garden in the back of the château. For the last two weeks she'd been dying to know how he was doing. Today she'd learned more during these few hours than she would have dreamed. He was so wonderful with Nadine, she could never thank him enough. There wasn't a man alive like him.

That's what made this so hard. He shouldn't have come. More memories had been made that would live with her forever. More pain to endure after they said goodbye.

Dinner arrived. They ate together, but Nadine fell asleep before she could finish. The day had worn her out, and Françoise helped her get ready for bed. Jean-Louis waited for her out in the hall.

"Do you sleep here now?" he asked when she joined him. "I discovered you gave up your job and your apartment in Paris."

She took a quick breath to combat her guilt.

"I rent a nearby apartment. She needs constant care now."

"How wonderful she has you. I'll follow you to your place. We have to talk."

"I wish you hadn't come, but since you're here, let's go out to my car. We can talk there."

He didn't argue with her, they left the building and got in her car. He'd parked next to her.

She trembled from his nearness. "You were so sweet to Nadine. It's obvious she enjoyed your visit very much."

"But you weren't happy to see me."

Françoise had never been more conflicted in her life. How could she answer his question honestly? She was desperately happy to see him. His kindness to Nadine only made that worse. She was in agony to be so near him. But she had to remain strong and resist, do everything she could to deter him. It had to be this way for his sake as well as for her own sanity.

"No. I told you I have to do my own thing from now on. Why on earth are you here?"

He turned to her. "It's called desperation. I called Claude Giraud. You wouldn't let me do it before, but I couldn't bear the separation from you. I ended up contacting him. He was able to obtain the information you need so badly so we can be together."

"What?" she cried in sheer disbelief.

"He tried to phone you, but couldn't reach you with the phone number I gave him. That's when I found out you were nowhere to be found. I went to your apartment, your work. No one could or would tell me anything. My one link to you was your great-aunt, so I came here today. For all I knew, you might have moved the two of you to some other town."

She pressed her hands to her face. "I don't believe what I'm hearing. How dare you go against my wishes! That wasn't your right, and I could never have afforded it. You've betrayed me! This means *you* know every painful, maybe even criminal thing my father might have done. Do you have any idea how much that hurts me?"

He groaned. "How could I hurt you? I was trying to erase your pain. Claude has told me nothing because it's not my business. But if you'll give me your new phone number, I'll pass it on to him. He'll call and tell you all that you want to know about your adoption.

It'll be between the two of you and no one else. Ever."

Her head reared. "Don't you understand what you've done? How could you go behind my back? I thought I could trust you."

"Don't you get it, Françoise? I did everything I could to bring us together because *I'm in love with you*!"

His declaration filled the interior of the car, shaking her to the foundations.

"I want to be your husband. I want to make love to you for the rest of our lives. I want to have children with you. The love I have for you will never go away. There's no other woman in the world for me. I came here fighting for a life with you. Only you. Nothing will make sense if you're not my other half."

He reached in his jacket pocket and drew out a card. "Since you can't bring yourself to give me your phone number, then you call Claude. It's up to you. He's ready to give you the answer you've been waiting for. Despise me if you want, but he put his life on the line to get this information for you." He put the card on the dashboard.

She'd started to shiver.

"I thought you felt the same way about me,

but I was wrong. You have my solemn promise that I'll never come near you again."

He climbed out of her car and turned to her. "I've already thanked you for saving my life, but at this moment I have to ask myself if it was worth it when it means I've lost you. I wish you and your great-aunt well in the future, Françoise." The door closed.

She hugged her arms to her chest, filled with soul-destroying shame over her reaction to his revelations. Only Jean-Louis could have given her such a priceless gift motivated by pure love. To her horror, she'd trampled all over it out of an irrational fear of the unknown.

And your own despicable pride, Françoise. A man as truly magnificent as Jean-Louis doesn't deserve a pitiful woman like you.

Long after she heard him drive away, she stumbled out of the car and hurried back to Nadine, dying inside.

Her godmother looked up and lifted a hand, as if to ask why Jean-Louis hadn't come in with her. He'd made a friend while they'd put that puzzle together.

"He's gone, Mame."

The older woman's hand holding one of the

little photos fell to the sheet and tears dripped down her pale cheeks.

Françoise sank down in the chair. *What have I done?*

CHAPTER EIGHT

JEAN-LOUIS HAD JUST come downstairs in jeans and a T-shirt when he saw his sister in the château foyer. "Corinne? If anyone needs me, I'll be at the garage."

She turned to him. "You don't want breakfast first?"

"Not now, thanks. I'm meeting the kids in a few minutes. We'll grab some food later."

"Everyone's excited you've had it rebuilt. Did you know that Honoré and Theo are dying to work with their Oncle Jean-Louis now that it's ready?"

"Old news, *ma soeur*. See you later."

A week ago he'd flown home after the disastrous confrontation with Françoise. His world had disintegrated before his very eyes. During the time he'd been home, he'd supervised the birth of the new garage. Jean-Louis had needed to keep so busy he wouldn't have time to think.

The building contractor who worked on the restored church/hospital for Nic had sent out more crew to help Jean-Louis. Now that school was out, his fifteen-year-old nephews had been pestering him to start working there. Maybe it was a genetic thing with some of the family that made them want to repair cars, trucks and tractors. He wondered what Françoise would make of—nope! That era was behind him.

He climbed in the new truck he'd bought in town to get around the estate. This morning he headed for the garage. While growing up, his old refuge had been a place of peace and pleasure for him. When Jean-Louis had first opened the creaky door after being gone a decade, he'd experienced an overpowering sense of nostalgia.

Beneath a dim light he'd looked around the big, empty relic. His old toolbox had been sitting there lifeless and untouched since he'd left for Paris with his brothers at eighteen. Where had the years gone?

Today he used the new remote to open the garage door. In seven days, the whole place had been transformed into a mechanic's state-of-the-art facility. He parked the truck and walked inside. Last evening he'd put one of the unreliable estate cars up on the lift for the boys to work on.

In a minute they appeared on their bikes. They hopped off and walked inside with huge smiles.

"Good morning, gentlemen. Right on time." They looked excited. Nothing like the soldiers Jean-Louis had been assigned to train in the army. No doubt at his nephews' ages, he'd worn the same goofy expression.

Honoré eyed the car. "Are we going to work on that old clunker?"

"How did you guess?"

"It hasn't run for a long time," Theo piped up.

"Then imagine how surprised everyone will be after you grease monkeys get it cranking again. Once you guys turn sixteen, it'll be your car to drive around in on the estate." Both of them had birthdays coming up.

They high-fived each other on a burst of pure happiness.

Jean-Louis walked over to the lift. He'd

forgotten what that kind of emotion felt like. In one week he'd turned into a hundred-year-old man.

At four thirty in the afternoon, Françoise finally found the deli she'd been looking for in La Racineuse. Needing sustenance after the flight from Bourges to Chalon Champforgeuil, she parked her rental car in front and hurried inside for coffee and a meat pie to take with her.

A few minutes later she ate on the way to the Causcelle château. Memories of the night she'd done the same thing with Jean-Louis en route to the hospital assailed her. She'd never known such happiness.

Her whole life had changed the first time she'd met Robert Martin. Yet a month and a half later, she'd done the unthinkable by wounding him and destroying what could have been divine happiness.

Françoise didn't expect forgiveness, let alone anything else. But she had to find him and bare her soul or she couldn't go on living. It would serve her right if he refused to see or talk to her. Still, she'd do whatever it took to convince him she never meant to hurt him. She wanted the chance to tell him he was the literal answer for her having been created.

The sight of the château hurt, because of all the wonderful memories Françoise had tried to put out of her mind. She pulled up in front, desperate to see and talk to Jean-Louis. After changing her mind half a dozen times, she'd chosen to wear a new periwinkle-colored silk blouse with pleated white pants.

She checked herself in the mirror. The little periwinkle earrings had been the right touch. When Jean-Louis told her she'd wasted her effort to come here, she wanted to have made a favorable impression before leaving.

Girding up her courage, she slid out of the car and hurried to the entrance. Two bikes stood outside. Before she could ring the buzzer, two teenage boys came bursting out the door. They stopped immediately when they saw her.

"Bonsoir," she greeted them. "I'm looking for Jean-Louis Causcelle. It's very important. Do you know if he's here?"

"He's over at the garage," the dark-haired boy answered her.

The famous garage. Jean-Louis was there.

She almost melted on the spot.

"Yeah," said the one with the blond hair. He carried a sack of something in his hand. "We're going there right now to take him dinner. Follow us."

They took off like speed demons. Overjoyed by this accidental meeting, she hurried back to the car and drove behind them a mile to the place on the estate he'd cherished. She saw a new truck parked outside, but the garage door was closed.

The blond boy got off his bike and knocked on the door. "Oncle Jean-Louis? Open up. Tante Corinne sent your dinner."

"Thanks, guys," came his deep voice. "Just leave it and I'll get it in a minute. Right now, I'm draining the oil pan."

"Okay."

"See you tomorrow, same time."

"Ciao!" they both called out.

"I'll see that he gets it," Françoise whispered to them.

They nodded and rode away, but kept looking back at her. She picked up the sack, wondering how long she'd have to wait. Her heart lodged in her throat. After a minute she grew so nervous she couldn't take it any longer.

Praying for help, she walked over to the door and knocked.

"I thought you guys had left."

In a moment the door lifted and she found herself three feet away from the most gorgeous male on earth. Oil covered parts of his face, T-shirt and arms. He'd been wiping his hands with a paper towel, but he stopped when he saw her.

"Jean-Louis—" she cried. "Please don't close the door on me yet. You would have every right, but I need to talk to you and beg your forgiveness. Then I promise I'll go away."

He didn't move. "How long have you been out here?"

"Just a minute. I drove to the château and your nephews were just leaving on their bikes. I asked if you were there and they said to follow them. This is your dinner." She started to hand the sack to him.

"I can't do anything until I get this oil washed off." His face had such an impassive look, her heart plummeted to her feet. This wasn't her Jean-Louis. "I'll meet you at home."

Still, one prayer had been answered. He

hadn't yet told her to get out of his life and stay out.

"Thank you."

On trembling legs, she got in the car and put down the sack before driving to the château. Before long Jean-Louis trailed behind her in his truck. He parked next to her near the entrance and they both got out.

The moment seemed surreal when he opened the front door for her. "Come upstairs with me where we can be private."

Another prayer had been answered because they didn't run into any of his family as they climbed to the second floor. She'd done this before, but he didn't stop at the suite she'd used on her first visit. He kept walking down the hall to his room and opened the door for them.

"Come in while I shower and change." After shutting the door, he turned on the TV in the sitting room and handed her the remote. "I won't be long."

Françoise sat down on the couch to wait. It was inconceivable that he'd let her into his suite when she'd been so cruel to him. She couldn't believe he would be this decent after what she'd said and done. His polite formality was killing her, yet decency was one of his many exceptional traits. She turned off the TV, unable to concentrate on anything and too anxious for the final confrontation,

"Do you want something to drink?"

She jumped up in surprise and turned around. Jean-Louis had come from the shower wearing a casual tan sport shirt and white cargo pants. The wonderful scent of the soap he'd used clung to his powerful body.

"I don't want anything, thank you, but you need to eat." She looked down at the couch. "Oh, no—your dinner is still in my car! I forgot."

"Don't worry. I'm not hungry."

She clasped her hands in front of her. "Jean-Louis? All I want to do is apologize until you believe that I never meant to hurt you." Her eyes swam with tears she couldn't prevent.

He rubbed the back of his neck. "I know it's not in you to hurt anyone deliberately."

A little moan escaped. "You don't have to pretend with me. What I did can never be forgiven. There's no excuse for the way I reacted when you told me about talking to Monsieur Giraud."

"You had every right to be furious, Françoise. I went against your wishes."

"But I know why you did it, and I've been out of my mind ever since for the unconscionable way I treated you."

"That's because you were traumatized the day you found that adoption paper."

A groan came out of her. "A mature woman doesn't act like that. In the beginning, my fears escalated out of control. When I met you, part of me was terrified that in learning something terrible about my father, you'd hear about it and I'd *lose* you!"

He moved closer. "Lose me? What are you talking about? I meant nothing to you."

"You're so wrong about that." His eyes narrowed, as if he hadn't heard her correctly. "When you asked me to lunch to repay me for saving your life, I was already so crazy about you, I couldn't think."

She heard his sharp intake of breath. "Say that again."

"I *want* to say it again. The truth is, I fell in love with you at the hospital in Nice."

After a long silence, "You're serious."

By now the tears had started running down her cheeks. "Unfortunately, up until a week ago I was too blind with fear to tell you I love you more than life itself. If my father had done something unpardonable, then it would taint me too and you would never want anything to do with me." Her voice broke.

"*That's* been at the root of your fear? That I'd reject you?" He sounded incredulous.

She clung to the end of the couch. "I've known losses in my life, but the thought of losing you meant my life would be over. I shrank from facing it."

"Françoise—"

She looked up. "That first night after drawing your blood, I went home and had dreams of the most gorgeous vampire in existence entering my room. It was *you*, Jean-Louis. You devoured me with those eyes of black fire and willed me into your powerful arms."

"You're making this up."

This man she adored didn't believe her. Maybe she'd done too much damage and he couldn't. "I swear I'm not. I ran to you and we started to make love. It wasn't enough. I begged you to bite me with your beautiful white teeth so we would live together forever."

He shook his head. "Do you hear what you're saying?"

She'd never seen him in shock before. It made her smile in spite of her tears. "I *know* what I'm saying. When I first awakened, I was giddy with joy to have been turned by you and I needed you desperately. But you weren't there! I was frantic to find you until I realized it had only been a dream. I'd never been so desolate in my life."

More fire flickered in his eyes. "I wish I'd been there," he teased. Her old Jean-Louis was finally coming out of shock.

"From that moment on, my palpable hunger for you frightened the daylights out of me so much, I purposely stayed away from you for that whole first week."

An enticing smile broke the corner of his compelling mouth. "I wondered why I hadn't seen hide nor hair of you. Now I understand the reason why you've always been running from me."

"You don't know the half of it. It only took one more time to lay my eyes on you, and I knew you were part of my heart, mind, blood and soul. I told myself that if I got away from you immediately, my fantasy would dissipate with time."

That deep chuckle of his escaped. "Did it work?"

Heat crept into her face. "You know it didn't. I never stopped willing you to come to me, not even when I was six hundred miles away from you."

"That was a great disappearance trick you pulled on me, Dr. Valmy."

"Disappearance nothing. Lo and behold, a few weeks later there was my vampire. I'd willed him to Paris and he'd found me, appearing out in front of the hospital. He drove a Mercedes, no less. You'd taken on a new identity in breathtaking human form, not even wearing hospital pajamas."

A dashing smile appeared. "Which version do you like better?"

"You're an amalgam of both I adore. As the clerk on the fifth floor had described, you were the hunkiest vet she'd ever seen in her life. I already knew that and wanted to scratch her eyes out along with Suzanne's because you were *mine*. I'd already drunk of your essence in my dream."

"Don't I wish. We're going to have to reenact

that particular dream right away." The throb in his voice resonated to her insides.

"I'll never forget it. We'd said our vows to each other during that night of impossible rapture no human could imagine. But again, I had to face the stark fact that being a human, I couldn't be with you. My earthly existence had been marred by an event of my parents' choosing, an event beyond my control."

Jean-Louis put his hands on her upper arms. "Which brings us to the matter of your adoption."

"But I'm not worried about that anymore."

Her words brought him up short. "You're not making sense."

"Listen to me, darling. On the evening after you left Silver Pines, I drove to my apartment and wrestled with my thoughts and emotions all night. By morning, I'd come to my senses with only one thought. Because of your sacrifice, you had risked everything so we could be together. The quote about greater love hath no man had been indelibly impressed on my soul. I realized nothing else mattered. As soon as I could, I flew here."

His hands squeezed her shoulders. "Then you mean—"

"I never called Monsieur Giraud," she broke in on him.

"But—"

"No *buts*. You did everything humanly possible to help me get my life back, yet I trampled all over yours. I'll spend the rest of my life showing you how sorry I am and how much I love you. The only important thing is to tell you I want to be your wife. I don't want to live without you." She slid her hands up his chest. "But only if you think you can forgive me."

"Forgiveness doesn't come into this." The tears in his voice told her everything.

"Oh, yes, it does. Don't you know I want to marry you as soon as possible? Do you still—?"

The rest of her words were smothered as his mouth closed over hers with a fierce hunger that had been building from the first moment they'd met. He wrapped his strong arms around her, enclosing her against his heart. They drank deeply, trying to show each other what they'd had to hold back for so long. She felt the imprint of his body run the length of hers. Desire exploded more potently than what she'd experienced in her dream.

"Darling," he cried, covering her face and hair with kisses. They were both out of breath.

"I love you, Jean-Louis. I love you. You couldn't possibly know how much." No kiss lasted long enough.

A new dream started as he picked her up like a bride and carried her to his bedroom. Once he lowered her to the bed, she got lost in the ecstasy of being able to show him her love. She had no cognizance of time while they were finally giving in to their passion. Then suddenly he groaned and pulled away from her, getting to his feet.

She gazed up at him. "What is it, Jean-Louis?"

"I'm so in love with you, I'm ready for this to be our wedding night, but it isn't. Not until we've said our vows and I've put my ring on your finger. And that can't happen until you've spoken with Claude."

She sat up and moved to the edge of the bed. "No, darling. I told you it doesn't matter."

"Yes, it does, deep down. While Claude is still alive and able to tell you everything, you need to hear it before the information is gone forever. Whatever you learn, I know you'll handle it and I'll be with you all the way. Be honest with yourself. Then we can plan our wedding with no shadow marring our happiness."

Jean-Louis had spoken from his heart, and those words reached her soul.

"You're right. You're always right." She checked her watch. "It's ten to ten. Do you think—?"

"He'll still be up."

"Will you stay in here with me? I want to do everything with you. We'll listen together."

He took a fortifying breath. "Do you still have that card?"

"No. I'm sorry, but I tore it up. You'll have to give me the number again. My phone is in my purse in the sitting room."

"Stay right there. I'll get it." He rushed out and came back in another minute with her purse. She pulled the phone out and handed it to him to program Claude's number from his phone.

After he gave it back to her, he sat on a chair near the bed and waited for her to call the agent. The loving smile Jean-Louis flashed gave her the confidence to go through with this. She pressed the digits and heard the voice mail say to leave a number. Françoise followed through.

"He'll call back, *mon amour.*"

Seconds after he'd spoken, her phone rang. She clicked on. "Monsieur Giraud?"

"Dr. Valmy. I wondered when I'd hear from you."

"There are no words to thank you enough for what you've done."

"The Causcelle family has been a good friend to me. I'm only happy to help. Are you ready?"

With the man she loved seated right in front of her, holding her hand, she was ready for anything. "Yes. Please tell me what you know."

"Your mother's birth name is Vivienne Fortin. She never knew her parents and was left inside a church in a blanket on a pew. She was taken to an orphanage in the village where she grew up. All the children attended church when old enough. In her teens she struck up a friendship with an altar boy from the village.

"They fell in love at seventeen, but fate stepped in and his family moved from the village. He never came back. She learned he'd been headed for the priesthood. Vivienne decided to become a nun. Before taking her final vows, she became ill and was sent to a regional hospital. Your father, Dr. Patrick Valmy, happened to be the intern on duty late that night.

"The initial examination proved she was near seven months along and in labor. He delivered a live baby. Her habit had hidden her pregnancy, so no one knew.

"She told your father she'd repented of her sin and could still be a bride of Christ. It was what she wanted with her whole heart and soul. Would he arrange for her daughter to be adopted? Since she'd never known her parents, she begged him to find her the best home possible with a loving mother and father. Then she confided her secret.

"The boy she'd loved was the grandson of a cardinal close to the pope in Rome. If word got out that his grandson was the baby's father, it would be disastrous for him, his family and the Church. Since he didn't know about the pregnancy, Vivienne wanted to spare the man she'd loved as much pain as possible.

"Your father sent her back to the nunnery, indicating she'd had a bleeding problem, but it had been corrected. He honored her wish by having her sick three-pound baby transported to a hospital in another city for expert care. Six weeks later that hospital sent the well baby to another orphanage.

"Your father and mother talked it over. Since she'd gone through three miscarriages, they would adopt this baby, which would be a blessing to everyone. Your parents applied for the adoption and brought you home. Your father slowly gathered all this information and wrote it down. At that point it was sealed by special order.

"To this day your birth mother and birth father are alive, serving God as a nun and as a priest in different areas on this planet. I'll say this, Dr. Valmy. Not every adopted child has such a lineage of earthly and spiritual parentage in their DNA. You're a blest woman to claim these four dedicated, saintly people as your parents. Your father wrote that he and your mother considered raising you as their sacred trust.

"Jean-Louis confided to me that you've been his savior. After what I've learned about your heritage, it doesn't surprise me. It's been my privilege to assist you both. My lips are sealed. I'll say good night." He clicked off.

Françoise broke down sobbing.

Jean-Louis stood up and pulled her into his arms. He brushed his lips over her wet face, only able to imagine her joy and wonderment. They clung for a long time. This answer meant their lives could begin, starting with a marriage ceremony he wished were happening this very second.

"You're my heaven-sent miracle, Jean-Louis. I wish we were man and wife right this minute. I need you closer," she cried, flinging her arms around his neck. He crushed her against him and she lifted her mouth to his. Their long-suppressed hunger for each other began to set off sparks until they reached flash point.

"That's one miracle we need to arrange for tomorrow," he murmured against her lips. "Since I can't take my hands off you, let's go back to the sitting room where I can try to think. I don't trust myself in the same space with you, least of all this one." After another scorching kiss, he let her go and walked into the sitting room.

She hurried after him. "Jean-Louis—"

He turned to her, but was afraid of giving in to the passion she'd aroused in him. "You heard what your father said, Françoise. Your parents considered you their sacred trust. I do too, and I want to do this right. You're going to have to help me."

After eyeing him for a soulful moment, she stood on tiptoe to kiss his cheek, then she sat down on the couch.

He drew a chair close to her. "I've dreamed of this day since I first looked into your lush green eyes that reminded me of the grass surrounding the château. Where do you want to be married, *mon coeur*?"

She smoothed a dark curl off her forehead. "With my parents gone, you're going to be my family and you belong to a big, loving one. If you could have your heart's desire, where would it take place?"

"Besides claiming you for my bride and selfishly wanting to live on the estate with you all our lives?" He drew in a deep breath. "I wish we could be married in the church here. Father Didier, a younger, modern-thinking priest, married Nic in a short ceremony the way my brother wanted it. My sisters told me about it. I envied him."

She laughed gently. "A short ceremony sounds perfect to me. So does living here with you. Please tell me we don't have to wait three weeks to allow for the banns."

"That won't be a problem." He couldn't stay away from her, and slid onto the couch, kissing her long and hard. "Your love has transformed me," he spoke at last. "I want a church wedding especially for you, but it isn't possible. Because of a long-standing hatred that a certain man on the estate has for our father, Nic had to arrange for his marriage to Anelise to be performed in the living room here. He would have married her in the church otherwise."

"How awful that one man could create that kind of enmity. I'm so sorry."

"We're all sorry about it. This man has sown seeds of discontent among some of the estate workers for years. While my father has been alive, not even my sisters' marriages could be performed in the church. Every wedding has taken place in the living room to avoid serious repercussions that the Causcelle family has already paid for in the past.

I'll tell you about that later. Not tonight. I'm too happy."

She looked into his eyes. "I hope you realize I'd love to be married downstairs in front of your mother's painting. It would be an honor."

Emotion took over. "You're an angel, Françoise." He kissed her again, needing to pour out his love for her. "But I'm thinking of another place. The weather is still perfect. It came to my mind while I was visiting you and your great-aunt. Let's go downstairs and I'll show you."

They left his suite and walked down the hall to the stairs, kissing several times before they reached the foyer. He drew her down another hallway that led to the rear entrance of the château. He flipped a light switch before they walked out on a large patio with wrought iron furniture. The outside lights illuminated a rose garden in full bloom.

"Oh, darling—" she gasped quietly. "This is like a dream. You can smell the heavenly scent of the roses."

"How would you like to be married out here with the family looking on? My mother started the original garden years ago. Papa kept it going after she died. You mentioned that your great-aunt loved roses. Do you think she'd like this setting for her precious Françoise? I know my father would."

He heard a cry before she hugged him until it hurt. "How did it happen that you came into my life? What did I ever do to be loved by you?"

"I'm still asking that same question about you. Since your great-aunt is your entire family now, I want her blessing. Her needs have to come first."

Françoise kissed his jaw. "Do you know she wept when I walked in her room and told her you'd gone? You won her over that day putting the puzzle together."

"I enjoyed it too. In fact, I've thought of nothing but you two ever since. There's an empty suite on the main floor across the hall from Papa's. We could fly her here, where she can convalesce in comfort indefinitely. Between you and Luca, she'd have all the medical help needed, plus the château staff."

Sobs shook her body while she clung to him. "You're so wonderful, you're unreal."

Emotion gripped him. "Don't get me started on you."

She lifted her head and covered his mouth with her own. "I wish there were another word I could say to let you know what you mean to me. I love you too much."

"I don't think there is such a thing as too much, not where my feelings for you are concerned. Let's go in the kitchen and grab a bite to eat while we plan. I'd like us to be married within a few days."

"Is that possible?"

"I don't see why not," he said as they went back inside the château. "We will be married in the eyes of God, which is most important to us, I think? The civil ceremony can follow later." He turned off the outside lights and led her to the kitchen. "The whole family except for your great-aunt lives on the estate, but we'll take care of her tomorrow."

He fixed them sandwiches and coffee. Her arrival had brought back his appetite. He was starving for food, for her, for the life they were going to have together.

They sat at the kitchen table. "Forgive me that we haven't even talked about your career yet."

She eyed him over the coffee cup. "I've been thinking about that too. When I drove into La Racineuse earlier today and stopped to eat, I passed the hospital where I tested the blood samples. Maybe they need an epidemiologist?"

He leaned toward her and kissed her cheek. "I'm way ahead of you. After we visit the priest in the morning, we'll fly in the family jet to Bourges to pick up your car. Once back at Bouzy, we'll get you moved out of your apartment. Nadine's going to be surprised when we take her from Silver Pines and drive her to Bourges. During the flight here, we'll make her as comfortable as possible."

"You think we can do all of that in one day?"

"Why not? Tomorrow night the three of us will sleep on the flight back here because I don't want to be separated from you ever again. Until the wedding you'll stay in your old suite."

She chuckled. "I was only here for one night."

"The room is yours until the wedding."

"Jean-Louis? No one in your family knows about us yet. This is going to come as a huge shock."

"My nephews would have spread the news of your arrival to everyone hours ago."

"I forgot about that. They were so cute."

"My gorgeous Vampira—I'll let you in on a little secret. The male members of our coven were expecting an announcement the night you came to take their blood."

"You can say that again," sounded another deep male voice. Both of them looked around to see Raoul, who'd come in the kitchen. Jean-Louis got up, recognizing a certain glint in his brother's eyes.

"You have the same goofy look on your face that Nic still wears around here." Raoul stared at Françoise. "Thank heaven you came when you did. None of us has known what to do with him. Papa was overjoyed after Theo and Honoré spread the news that you'd arrived."

Her gentle laugh filled the kitchen. "It's a good thing no one was around me before *I* flew here."

He grinned. "Welcome to the family, Dr. Valmy."

"Please call me Françoise!"

"Entendu. How soon is the wedding?" He poured himself a cup of coffee.

Jean-Louis put his hands on her shoulders. "As soon as Father Didier can do the honors. Hopefully in a few days. We'll be meeting with him in the morning."

Raoul nodded. "Another Causcelle non-church wedding." He eyed Françoise. "I presume he's told you why."

"Only some of it, *frérot*," Jean-Louis responded for her. She didn't need to hear about Dumotte. Not yet. He leaned down to kiss the side of her neck. "It's late and you must be exhausted. If you've finished eating, why don't you go up to your room? I'll run out to the car for your suitcase and bring it to you. Did you lock it?"

"No. I only had one thing on my mind when I drove up to the château. I couldn't believe you hadn't told me to go away and never come back."

"I can promise you one thing. That will never happen, not in all eternity," he whispered. "I'm still in a daze. It's a miracle I'm even functioning. That's all because of you, my love." After another kiss on the back of her neck, he walked over to Raoul. "Come with me. I need to tell you our plans."

Raoul smiled at her. "Good night, Françoise, and congratulations. My brother is a lucky man."

"Thank you, Raoul. He's my life! As for marrying into your marvelous family, I'm the lucky one. I never had brothers or sisters. Now I'll have both. Nothing could thrill me more. *Bonne nuit.*"

After they left the kitchen, Françoise cleared the table and did the few dishes. Eighteen hours ago, she couldn't have imagined standing here in the château kitchen planning her marriage to the most wonderful man on earth.

No sooner had she gone upstairs and entered the suite she'd slept in before when she heard a knock on the door. Her heart leaped. "Come in."

"I don't dare. I'm leaving the suitcase outside the door with your purse and phone. Call me in the morning when you're awake and we'll drive to the church. I can't get married soon enough."

"I love you, Jean-Louis. I hope I don't wake up to find this has all been a dream like my first one where you vanished."

"That couldn't happen, *mon tresor.* We took vows in your dream, remember?"

She ran to open the door, wanting one more kiss from him, but he'd already disappeared down the hall. Françoise brought the case and her purse inside and quickly got ready for bed.

By some miracle she did fall asleep, but she woke up at seven the next morning so excited, she rushed to shower and wash her hair. Today she wanted to look perfect and chose to wear a light blue two-piece summer suit. The periwinkle earrings matched. After putting on lipstick, she slipped on high heels and felt ready.

As she reached for her phone, it rang. Jean-Louis! She clicked on. "Darling?"

"My prayer has been answered. You didn't run away from me."

She clutched her phone tighter. "I'm all ready to run away with you right this minute. Where are you?"

"In the foyer."

"I'm coming down."

Françoise grabbed her purse. She flew out the door and down the stairs. Jean-Louis caught her in his arms. "You're a dazzling sight." He kissed her so thoroughly, she lost her breath. "We'd better go or I'm going to take you back upstairs, *mon amour*."

They left the château in one of the estate cars. He reached for her hand. "I'm taking you to my favorite café for a celebration breakfast first. They serve the specialty of this local region, *saucisse de Montbéliard* with sensational Montbéliard *crème* and eggs."

"With one exception at the *palais*, breakfast has been the only meal we've ever sat down to," she teased.

"It's my favorite meal of the day." He squeezed her hand.

"I'll have to remember that. Since meeting you, it has come to be mine too."

The charming, family-owned café owner treated Jean-Louis like the prince she believed him to be. They were shown to his regular table. While they waited for his favorite food, he pulled something from the breast pocket of the immaculate dove gray suit he wore. He was so incredibly handsome she couldn't help staring at him.

Françoise didn't realize what he'd done until he'd reached for her left hand. She looked down and let out a small cry as he put a diamond ring on her finger. Not just any diamond. It was pear-shaped and probably three carats in the most glorious plush green color she'd ever seen.

He rubbed her palm with his thumb. "Now you know how I felt when I first looked into your eyes above the mask."

She'd never seen anything like it except in museums. He'd paid a king's ransom for it. "Oh, Jean-Louis. How did you get it in such a short amount of time? Did you have it with you when you came to the rest home before I ruined everything?"

He winked at her. Something he'd never done before. "There have to be some perks to being a billionaire."

At that moment the waitress brought their order while she sat there dazed. After the woman walked away, Françoise reached for his hand across the small table. "I love it." Her voice trembled. "I love you beyond comprehension." Tears filled her eyes. "I'll cherish this forever."

"I plan to cherish you forever. Now we're ready to meet the priest."

He began eating his food with relish. She ate, but she kept watching the way the diamond sparkled with every movement her hand made. The beauty of it fascinated her all the way to the church, where they were shown into the priest's office. Jean-Louis introduced her to Father Didier.

"We're anxious to be married as soon as possible. Like Nic, whom you married recently, our ceremony will have to take place at the château. We've planned to say our vows on the patio. How soon could you perform the wedding? It would be at your convenience, whether morning, noon or evening."

Françoise adored her husband-to-be. He was so eager he hadn't given the priest time to talk or even ask questions.

A smile broke out on the priest's face. "You not only look like your brother, you're as excited as he was. I've never seen two men more anxious to become husbands." His gaze flicked to Françoise. "But after meeting you and Mademoiselle Lavigny, I have a perfect understanding. Here's my dilemma."

Jean-Louis gripped her hand tighter.

"I'm leaving for church business today and tomorrow. On the following day when I return, which could be late, the ceremony would have to take place in the evening. Shall we say seven?"

"We can't ask for more than that, Father."

He lifted a hand. "I know you want it short. Would you like to say your own vows? I'll just officiate."

Françoise had never seen her fiancé beam before. "The Church needs more priests like you, Father. We'd love it."

"How do you feel about that, Dr. Valmy?"

"Jean-Louis and I are in total accord on everything. You're so kind to arrange your schedule for us."

"It'll be my pleasure. I'm glad you came when you did. I'll be leaving in a few minutes."

"Then we won't take up any more of your time. We'll see you on Wednesday evening, Father." Jean-Louis reached for Françoise and they left the office. Before he helped her in the car, he pulled her in his arms and buried his face in her hair. "I don't know about you, but I'm considering going back to church again."

Her laughter got smothered when he covered her mouth with his own. There was a little boy inside this remarkable man she loved with unleashed intensity. The thought of giving birth to a son like him one day thrilled the very daylights out of her.

CHAPTER NINE

THE FLIGHT TO Bourges from Chalon Champforgeuil on the private jet only took an hour. The drive in Françoise's car to Bouzy took fifteen minutes longer, but pure, unadulterated joy filled Jean-Louis's being. While Françoise drove, he talked on the phone with the rest of his family to make final arrangements. His father sounded elated and spoke to her, welcoming her officially to the family.

She stopped at the apartment. While she talked with the landlady and took care of the rent and lease money owing, he carried the few belongings out to her car.

Now to go to the rest home. He could only hope that in time her great-aunt would be happy with this move. When they walked in her room a little while later, she looked up at both of them from the bed.

"Triplet." She pointed to him.

"Yes, Mame. Jean-Louis is now my soon-to-be husband." She walked over to kiss her and show her the ring.

"Ah." The older woman's breath caught.

Françoise reached for the puzzle on the overbed table and tapped on the picture of the Causcelle Château. "We're going to live here, and we want you to live with us. Will you come?"

Jean-Louis could tell it took time for everything to register. He moved closer. "I love Françoise and want her to be happy. You're Françoise's family, and I love you too. We won't be happy if you don't come to live with us. Please say you will, Nadine, and you'll make me the happiest man on the planet." He tapped the château on the lid again. "We'll be getting married out by the rose garden, where you can see everything."

His heart thundered in his chest. This was the moment he'd been worried about. What if she didn't want to leave Silver Pines?

While he waited for a response, Nadine smiled and put her hand on his. Françoise stared at him in utter bliss. Nothing could prevent a happy marriage now. A new degree of joy seeped inside him. At that moment he remembered what she'd said to him in Mercy Hospital.

"So, you really do want to live! Wonderful! In that case you'll have to come for a phlebotomy every three months to keep levels normal. You'll need treatment throughout your life because there is no cure, but it should be a whole long life and a rich one."

By seven that evening, they'd eaten and boarded the jet for the flight to Chalon Champforgeuil. Earlier Jean-Louis had called ahead for a local ambu-car service that drove them to Bourges. Françoise left her car in the rest home parking area to be collected later.

They made her great-aunt comfortable for the flight. Once in the air, he turned to Françoise. "Raoul will meet us at the airport and drive us to the château. He told me our sisters are getting the suite ready for Nadine. When we arrive, she can go straight to bed."

Françoise turned to him with her heart in her eyes. "You and your family are heaven-sent. I'll spend the rest of my life trying to repay you for everything."

"Just keep loving me. It's all I'll ever want."

"That's my wish too. Darling? Tonight I

think I'd better spend the night with Nadine in her room."

"I was going to suggest it so she won't be nervous. Though she doesn't know it, she makes the perfect chaperone to keep me away from you."

A chuckle escaped. "That works both ways. Do you know what amazes me? She's managing so well despite her illness."

"She reminds me of Papa, who has rallied somewhat. You're the one who said happiness could bring on rejuvenation."

"I know one thing," Françoise commented. "Happiness radiated from her when she saw you walk in her room earlier. That means more to me than you'll ever know. She saw me baptized, and now she's going to see me married to the man in my dream. You're my one and only," her voice trembled. "If we do have a son one day, I want to name him Robert Martin Valmy Causcelle."

Jean-Louis loved the sound of that. "Maybe we'll have twins. I'd like the second one to be named Alain."

"And if another miracle happens and we have triplet sons, what do you want to name our third one?" she prodded him.

"Don't you know already?" he asked with a smile.

"I know what I'd like, but I want to hear *your* choice."

"I'll tell you on our wedding night."

She groaned. "That's two nights away—I love you so much it sounds like a lifetime."

"Don't I know it."

After the long wait, Wednesday evening arrived. Everyone had assembled out on the patio, where candles flickered in the perfumed night air.

Françoise had bought a knee-length wedding dress in town the day before. Nic's wonderful wife, Anelise, had gone with her. They'd both loved the vintage lace she'd found with a high neck secured at the back. The dress had long lacy sleeves and an A-line skirt that flared from the waist with a lace border at the hem. She'd felt it was a dress her mother and her birth mother would love too. After looking at several veils, she'd decided not to wear one.

Jean-Louis had sent her white roses to carry. He'd also sent a white rose corsage for Nadine to wear.

Feverish with excitement after doing her makeup, she slipped on new white satin high heels and left the room carrying her sheaf of flowers. Corinne's husband, Gaston, stood in the foyer filming her as she descended the staircase.

To her surprise, she found Louis waiting for her in his wheelchair. Though he had heart disease, he looked dapper in a navy dress suit with a white rose in his lapel. He smiled up at her. "I'm sorry your father isn't here. If you'll allow me, I'd consider it a privilege to escort you down the aisle."

Tears smarted her eyes. "I'd be honored."

With Luca pushing him, they started down the other hall to the rear of the château. "I never thought I'd live to see the day my Jean-Jean came home, let alone watch him marry a woman as angelic as my Delphine."

His words touched her to her soul. So did the revelation that he'd called his son *Jean-Jean*. "I love you, Louis." She squeezed his shoulder gently before they moved out to the patio. Among his sisters and their families, her great-aunt sat in her own wheelchair. Louis joined Corinne and her family. Father

Didier stood waiting in his traditional wedding vestments.

Next to him stood her gorgeous Jean-Louis wearing a navy dress suit and white shirt like his father. He too wore a white rose in the lapel. She walked up to join her fiancé, whose eyes were like flame as they played over her. Brigitte, Corinne's daughter, took the roses from her.

Father Didier opened his arms wide. "Once again, we've all come together for a very sacred occasion. This time to join Jean-Louis Ronfleur Causcelle and Marie Françoise Valmy in holy matrimony. God intended for us to live in families and cherish each other. This evening I see a perfect example in front of me.

"The bride and groom have asked to say their own vows and exchange rings now. I'm honored to be here to officiate.

"Françoise? If you'll turn to Jean-Louis and tell him what's in your heart."

By now hers was so full, she could hardly breathe, let alone get the words out. She gazed at him. "Less than two months ago, I met you, Jean-Louis. You were a vet at the hospital where I was finishing my fellowship in

Nice. You thought you were dying of an illness you'd contracted in Africa.

"Unbeknownst to you, I was going through the greatest trauma of my life. I'm convinced now we were supposed to meet by some divine plan because you were the answer to my every prayer. Not to mention that you're such an unbelievable specimen of the perfect man, you're the answer to every maiden's prayer."

Chuckles erupted from his family.

"Your kindness and love for others, your selfless generosity is so inspiring that I want you to know it's a privilege to be loved by you. Few women on this earth will ever know the joy I feel. I can't wait to have a family with you. As your wife, I vow to love and cherish you today and throughout all eternity. I want to give you this ring as a token of my love and fidelity."

Françoise reached for his hand and slipped the gold wedding band she'd bought yesterday on his ring finger. She knew it had surprised him when she heard his quick intake of breath.

Father Didier spoke next. "Jean-Louis, if you'll turn to Françoise and tell her what's in your heart."

She saw her beloved swallow hard.

"Less than two months ago I entered Mercy Hospital in Nice believing I was dying, and I wanted to die. I knew I'd been a failure as a human being to my family and feared it was too late for me to find redemption. I decided it was good I'd reached the end of my life.

"Then you came into my room, Françoise, and told me I wasn't going to die. You said I had a blood disorder, and you promised me I'd live a long rich life if I followed your instructions.

"Your mask hid your face, but not your eyes, which were green like the fields of paradise. I looked into those eyes and thought I'd been transported to heaven. After you helped put me on the path to health, you left for Paris. That's where we met again, but there was no mask this time. Believe me, the goddess Aphrodite has nothing on you."

More happy sounds came from the family.

"I vow to love and cherish you forever. I long to be your husband, to take care of you in sickness and in health. I want to have children with you. I thank God for you, Françoise." He reached for her left hand and slid a gold wedding band next to her engagement ring. Then he leaned over unexpectedly and kissed her hand. It was a gesture only he would think to do. She almost melted on the spot.

Father Didier smiled as he looked at the two of them. "May the Lord in his kindness strengthen the consent you have declared before the Church. May He graciously bring to fulfillment his blessings within you.

"By the authority vested in me, I now pronounce you husband and wife. What God has clearly joined together, let no man put asunder. In the name of the Father, the Son and the Holy Spirit. Amen."

In the next breath Jean-Louis swept her in his arms and gave her a husband's kiss. This was where she'd longed to be. It sent electricity through her body as she clung to him and forgot everything else.

While deep in Jean-Louis's embrace, she heard Father Didier say, "I don't think this groom needs to be told what to do next, do you?" More chuckles ensued from their audience. "If you'll notice, the first Causcelle son to be married got carried away just like Jean-Louis. I know they're both part of a set of triplets, but they're even more alike than I thought."

Laughter exploded, causing her husband to lift his head while she blushed. Father Didier cleared his throat. "Members of the Causcelle family, I have the honor to present Monsieur *et* Madame Causcelle."

Everyone clapped and gathered round to wish them happiness. Nic and Raoul gave them special hugs. Her new husband belonged to an exclusive triumvirate. Next came his father, who hugged him, followed by the rest of the family.

Luca wheeled her great-aunt over so Françoise could kiss her. Then Honoré and Theo walked up to their uncle. "You'll be working in the garage with us tomorrow, right?"

Jean-Louis grinned. "Afraid not. I'll see you two characters on Monday."

Brigitte stood behind them. "You guys— they'll be on their *honeymoon*!"

"Zut!" they both said at the same time and walked over to the buffet table to eat.

Françoise tried hard not to laugh, but she couldn't help it. Jean-Louis grabbed her around the waist from behind. "Welcome to *our* family," he whispered against her ear. They *were* her family now. She loved them. "It's time we went upstairs, where our own private feast is waiting, Madame Causcelle. One day we'll take a honeymoon to some exotic place," Jean-Louis promised.

"I'm glad we're not going anywhere. The château feels like home to me already. It's a blessing that Nadine seems so happy. Did you see her and your father putting a puzzle together yesterday?"

"Luca knows what he's doing. Now it's our turn, *ma belle*."

When they reached the foyer, he caught her up in his arms and carried her effortlessly up the stairs and down the hall to his suite. "We'll have this wing to ourselves until we build our own home." He opened the door and closed it with his foot before carrying her through to the bedroom. She kicked off her high heels on the way.

"Since meeting you I've dreamed of keeping you prisoner in this room that became my childhood haven once I could sleep in a bed. But until I came back from Africa without hope, I had no idea the best part of my life was yet to happen," he cried, lowering her to the floor. "I can't believe you're my wife! I love you so much I'm in pain with it. Help me, darling."

"My dress fastens at the back of my neck."

She felt him reach around. "Whoever designed this piece of temptation made sure the groom went through agony first."

How she adored him! "I'm in my own agony waiting for my groom to figure it out." His impatience delighted her. She kissed his jaw. "I thought you were a mechanic."

"Maybe I'll just rip it off you."

"Ooh. I can see you haven't had practice on this sort of problem. Let the doctor do it." She reached behind her and undid the four hooks and eyes in an instant. Her dress slid down.

"Françoise—"

Sunlight filtered through the windows when Jean-Louis woke up. His beautiful dark-haired wife was draped across his chest, sound asleep. After the indescribable night of loving each other into oblivion, he wanted to know that rapture over and over again.

He raised up on one elbow to study the exquisite, giving woman he'd married. How was it possible he'd met his soul mate at the very darkest moment of his existence? When she'd spoken her vows to him last evening, she'd talked about a divine plan that had brought them together. That's what it had to be.

Unable to resist, he slid his fingers into her hair, needing to touch her. The thought of ever being apart from her killed him. He didn't even want to think about the pain his father must have gone through when he lost his wife. But he needed to stop dwelling on his fear of losing Françoise. He'd been given the most precious gift imaginable and would always relish this living, breathing miracle who was his wife.

All of a sudden, he felt her stir. She made a strangled sound.

He cradled the back of her neck. "Darling?"

She thrashed around, obviously still in a deep sleep. "I can't find you," she cried out. "Jean-Louis—where are you? Don't vanish on me. I'll die if you don't come back to me. Where have you gone?" By now she was virtually sobbing tears.

That dream she'd had before…

"Sweetheart! Wake up!" He pulled her into his arms and covered her wet face with kisses. "I'm here, my love."

Those heavenly green eyes slowly opened. She stared at him in disbelief. "You're here!

Thank heaven, thank heaven." She threw her arms around his neck and clung to him for dear life.

Eventually the tears subsided and she looked at him. "We were in paradise, and then you disappeared like you did before."

"That was a dream, Françoise. When you told me about the first one you experienced in Nice, I had trouble believing you, but not anymore. Just know that before you go to sleep in my arms every night from now on, I'll be here when you wake up. I may not be a vampire, but we're bonded forever. You'll never be able to escape me."

"I don't want to escape. Not ever. Love me again." She kissed him as only she knew how, thrilling him to his very core. To think he had this to look forward to whether waking or sleeping all the days of their lives was beyond his comprehension.

Another hour of bringing immeasurable pleasure to each other, and she brushed her fingers across his jaw. "You need a shave, my love, and I know we both need to eat. But before we budge from this bed where I've known rapture, I want to confide something to you."

His black eyes danced. "Are we pregnant?"

She chuckled. "Don't I wish."

He kissed the corner of her mouth. "Is it a secret?"

"No. It's something your father said on the way out to the patio last evening. The tender sweetness in his tone caught at my heart."

"Now I'm really intrigued."

"He said, 'I never thought I'd live to see the day my Jean-Jean came home, let alone watch him marry a woman as angelic as my Delphine.'" She sat up. "He called you Jean-Jean. For one moment I caught a glimpse of the father he'd been when you were his little boy. I'm so thankful you made it home in time for the two of you to pour out your love to each other again."

His eyes glistened with unshed tears. "I only wish he had enough time to see our children born."

"Well, that settles it. If we have triplets, one must be called Louis."

He crushed her in his arms. "Have I told you how much I love you? I've been thinking about the names if we have triplet girls. Our first will be Dionne in honor of the mother who raised the perfect daughter."

She kissed his chin. "We'll call the second one Delphine for the beautiful mother in that portrait downstairs."

His arms tightened. "And the third one we'll name Vivienne for the angel mother who gave you birth and made my world complete. A divine plan if there ever was one. Before we do anything else, I need to love you again, Françoise."

"If I had my way, we'd never leave this bed. Come here, my darling Jean-Louis."

* * * * *

Look out for the next story in the
Sons of a Parisian Dynasty trilogy

Coming soon!

And if you enjoyed this story, check out
these other great reads from
Rebecca Winters

Capturing the CEO's Guarded Heart
Second Chance with His Princess
Falling for the Baldasseri Prince

All available now!